MEN LIE WOMEN LIE

CHASTAÉ COLLINS

EDITOR
KAREN REDLACK

Acknowledgments

God, I owe it all to you! Thank you for making me the way that I am and for all the opportunities to do so many things. God, I thank you for all the good and bad things that I have been through that have lead me to this moment. To my family, the support and excitement you all have shared with me during this process has been heartfelt and very much appreciated. You all are truly my hype men and my motivation. Thank you so much to my editor Karen Redlack and SelfpublishMe in Oklahoma City for making my first book an easy transition. You all were very professional and provided great service. Thank you Alizjah for taking my vision and turning it into my cover art, I'm so proud of you. To my smart, educated, stylish, God fearing mother, Carla, it is an honor to be your daughter. Thank you for raising me. To my readers, thank you for taking the time to read my book. I hope you enjoy.

Dedicated to anyone suffering from depression, anxiety, PTSD, or personality disorders.

Mental Health Awareness:
Call 1-800-273-TALK (8255) or text MHA to 741741

National Suicide Prevention Lifeline:
1-800-273-8255

Visit www.psychologytoday.com to find a therapist near you.

CHAPTER 1

It was July 25th, a hot summer night in Oklahoma City (OKC). I was out with my friends Jessica and Lexi and we were celebrating my 30th birthday in downtown Bricktown. My birthday was Wednesday, but we decided to turn up this weekend. My name is Bre. My girls had dragged me out the house for a day of fun. First we went and got our nails and toes done, then they treated me to a fancy meal at Vast Restaurant on the top floor of Devon Tower. I was feeling cute and tipsy. I had on a black and white catsuit with red heels and red lips. I'm dark skinned, peanut butter thick, standing at 5'9" and about 6' in heels. A few guys had come up to me and was calling me a stallion. I would just smile, soaking up the attention I wasn't used to getting. Jessica, my bestie since middle school, stood at the same height and had the same skin tone. Jessica was slimmer, more of a model build, but every time we were together people always thought we were sisters ever since we were kids. It would always make me smile when people thought that because Jessica had the prettiest skin and most beautiful smile, but we might as well have been sisters cause she was my day uno and we will always be there for each other. At the club the DJ yelled, "If you team cancer and it's your birthday month put yo motha fuckin hands up and make some noise!" Lexi grabbed my hand and held it in the air and we all yelled from the top of our lungs. Then the DJ played 'Twerk' by City Girls and Cardi B. Next thing I know we were throwing our asses every which way on the dance floor. Lexi was extra turnt, she was damn near on the ground on all fours twerking. Lexi was about 5'7" caramel skin and what I call the 'wild child' out of the three of us. Lexi was real pretty and had had her ass and breasts done about a year ago and she was always drawing attention from men everywhere we went. I met Lexi in college at University of Central Oklahoma and we been cool ever since.

I usually was the one in the group always in a relationship, but as of two weeks ago, I was newly single. I was in a three year long toxic relationship and I was glad to finally had found the strength to leave. Although still heart broken, I was determined to move on. Jessica yelled in my ear over the music, "I'm glad you came out with us tonight, fuck Drew, you deserved better." I rolled my eyes, "Don't even bring him up." Jessica still yelling, "I'm just saying don't ever waste your time with his hoe ass again, his ass is for the STREETS!" Lexi yelled "PERIODDTTTT!" I laughed at Lexi, "Aye Lexi chill out." Jessica looked at Lexi concerned, "Yeah how many drinks have you had?" Lexi leaned in close to us and said, "I've had five... times four," Lexi laughed at herself. Jessica and I glanced at each other remembering what happened the last time we were out with Lexi and she had one too many drinks. Let's just say that night ended with wigs being snatched and somebody's tire being put on flat, but that was back in our hardcore partying days. We were grown now. Me and Jessica were 30 and Lexi was 29. We went back to our table that we had reserved and I mingled with some old friends that I hadn't seen in a while. Lexi walked over to me almost rolling her ankle, "What's up with the after party? We going to Ice Event Center?" Bre interjected, "Girl I'm going home and going to sleep. I'm already feeling sleepy, but I am down for some Waffle House." Lexi rolled her eyes and looked at Jessica and before she could ask her Jessica said, "Uh un I work in the morning." Lexi got sad, "Come on y'all never go out with me, let's live it up tonight." Me and Jessica wasn't giving in. Lexi got mad, "Y'all some old ass ladies bro." Jessica shrugged her shoulders and I agreed, "Ya damn right hun-tee, I will be going home, popping this bra off and letting these titties loose in my old lady nightgown." Jessica laughed and slapped me five. I used to be able to party like that, but my body and knees wouldn't allow it. Lexi went over to another mutual friend that was with us, probably to see what she had going afterwards. I shook my head. *That girl can party!*

Lexi was always down for whatever. You needed her to fight, she was ready. You needed her to sell somebody's grandma some weed, she was on it. And not to mention she was the plug on all the latest shoes, clothes, and accessories. Some would say she was shady and full of drama, but she was my girl and has had my back since college. My girl Jessica was always grinding, she kept two jobs since she was 17. Jessica had plans on buying a house and retiring early while living comfortable with her eight year old daughter, Anya, who was her biggest motivation. Jessica and her baby daddy, Eric, were not together but they co-parent peacefully without any drama, something you don't hear about much. They were both determined to raise Anya in a healthy, stable environment, as much as they could and they were doing a great job. Me and Lexi did not have any kids. Lexi said she didn't want any. I wanted to have a family someday with the right man and the clock was ticking.

I was, for the most part, low key. I was more of a homebody, but still enjoyed a good time. Unfortunately, these last three years had been more work than play due to all the energy I had put into my career. I was one of the top five therapists in Oklahoma City. I always wanted a career in helping others and I love connecting with people on a deep emotional level. I hated small talk, I wanted to learn about why you think and feel the way you do. Let's talk about past traumas and how to heal from them. And here I am currently on the dance floor twerking like my life depended on it, having the best time ever. As I celebrated my 30th I thought how my life has been mostly boring and I wanted to change that and bring some excitement into my life and try to be more open in saying yes instead of no. Little did I know excitement was going to find me.

CHAPTER 2

I woke up at home in my bed, slightly hung over, and thighs sore from dancing all night. After we left the club we went to eat and surprisingly Lexi came back home with us. We were out 'til three in the morning. I checked my phone for the time and it was 10:30 AM. The girls had stayed the night at my place. Jessica had already left to go to work and Lexi was on the couch. I stretched and got up and went to the bathroom to pee. While I was sitting on the toilet I could hear Lexi whispering on the phone. The conversation sounded a little aggressive like maybe she was arguing with someone. Then I heard her say "ok, ok, just give me a week and I'll handle it." Without realizing it, I was damn near leaning off the toilet trying to hear what she was saying. I got up, washed my hands, and pulled my braids into a bun. My small, butt length, knotless, box braids were courtesy of the duo Erica Diggs and Brianna Pendleton down at OKC Braids on NW Expressway. I took a shower and didn't think much of Lexi's conversation. Knowing her, she was caught up on some BS, get rich quick scheme. I never understood how someone could live their life like that, constantly searching for the next dollar instead of just getting a legit steady income. Seemed stressful to me, but I never judged her cause she was my girl and she was a grown ass woman.

After I showered, I washed my face. I had been taking extra care of my skin and it was glowing and looking youthful. "Ha 30 where bih?" I said and stuck my tongue out and looked back as I twerked in the mirror. I got dressed in some jean shorts and a black tee that had black queen on the front and my black pumas. I put on my fav Fenty lip gloss and full frontal mascara. Lexi walked into my room as I was letting my braids down, "Hey what you got up for today?" "I'm starving so I'm gonna go grab brunch and probably lounge for the rest of the day. Wanna go eat with me?" Lexi hesitated at first "Nah imma go link up with current bae this month," she laughed at herself. I said, "Who Johnny?" "Nope," she giggled. I continued guessing "DJ?" Her face twisted up and she rolled her eyes "I gave him some and he was on point for about a good 63 seconds and next thing I know he was singing like Jodeci." I was bent over laughing. She continued, "Then he had the nerve to say he hadn't ate and didn't have any energy. I was like, boy if you don't getcho 'gas tank on E' ass out my house with them excuses." We both laughed. It was the 63 seconds for me. "Well girl, I'm bout to head out, you sure you don't want to go, it's on me." Lexi never turned down free food, shidd who did. She asked, "Where you going?" "I'm going to First Watch on Memorial." "Oh ok, I'll pass, thanks though." I shrugged my shoulders, grabbed my purse, and we headed for the door. She got in her red mustang, fiddled around in her car and drove off. I hoped in my cherry jeep, "Oh shit, my mask."

It was the year 2020 and all hell had broken loose. We had lost Kobe in January and it seemed to go downhill from there. We were in a pandemic. CoronaVirus, aka COVID-19, aka "da rona" had come to the U.S. and messed everybody's life up. Hundreds of thousands had lost their lives. Although I had risked it all last night for my 30th, I had been locked up at home since late March. I mostly left the house for work, groceries, and occasional small family visits. I also offered virtual visits, but for those who would rather come to my office, masks were required. Quarantine life forced us to be in our heads to deal with personal and family trauma. It was at this time that I started to build up the strength to leave Drew. A lot of people could no longer be in denial about their anxiety and depression and my clientele increased. Also, a lot of people realized their job wasn't as secure as they thought it was. To be essential or nonessential, that was the question of the year. And the fact that there were arguments and fights about people's right to wear a mask was the most ridiculous shit I had ever heard.

I was in my car cruising on the way to eat with the AC blasting, it was 92 degrees, and Oklahoma has hot humid summers. I was taking in the view of the north side and all the people out and about. I had been living in OKC since I graduated from high school and I enjoyed living here. I pulled up to the restaurant and walked in. I let the server know a table for one. I had no problem eating alone. I actually enjoyed it. It was my "me time" and part of the many self-care habits I practiced. The host sat me at a booth. I ordered an omelet and a slice of french toast and enjoyed every bite. I sat at the table for a while after I finished eating and scrolled through social media. I paid for my meal and left a tip. As I was walking out the door towards my car, I noticed a guy looking all around my car. What the hell? "Excuse me can I help you?" I asked with an attitude. I stopped dead in my tracks realizing I shouldn't get too close to him, didn't know if he was crazy or not. However, I was close enough to get a good look at him and he was sexy as hell. He looked up at me. He had a milk chocolate complexion without a pimple or scar in sight and he was rocking waves and a beard. His beard looked so soft, I just wanted to reach out and touch it. He had muscles every damn where and he had the strong nose of an African king and lips that were ready to be kissed by my other lips. And to top it all off he was dressed like he had just finished a photoshoot. All of a sudden Saweetie 'My Type' started playing in my head, THAT'S MY TYPE BABY THAT'S MY TYPE! He took a second to check me out also then said, "My bad I don't mean to look like a creep, the wind blew my mask somewhere over here and it's my last one." As he talked I noticed he had a dimple. I was thinking, damn just take my panties neowwww! "Oh," was all I could say. My shyness had started to settle in. Around people I didn't know I was quiet, I had to get a feel for you because everyone doesn't deserve you or your time, plus I like to get to know people and then ease my weirdness out a little at a time. But if you were to ask my close friends and family they would probably say I was talkative, goofy, and maybe a little hyper. One thing about me for sure I was always over analyzing and over thinking. After a few moments of awkward silence he said, "How was the food?" "What?" He snapped me out of my daydream I was having about him. He laughed and repeated, "How was the food, you just came out of there right?" he pointed to the restaurant. "Oh yeah, it was good," I replied. I was just still caught off guard on how fine he was. There was a voice in my head screaming Bitch get yo shit together before you miss out! He broke the awkward silence again, "I'm Blu, I just moved to the north side." "Nice to meet you, I'm Bre. What side of town you coming from?" "I'm coming from Midwest City. You know any good places to eat around here?" he said, as he stepped a little closer to me. I tried to play it cool, but I was smiling way harder than I should have been. "Yeah, I know a couple spots, what type of food do you like?" He laughed "Allofum," he continued, "I'm free this weekend, we could go somewhere to eat if you like." Anxiety knocked at my door, you don't know him, say no, but at the same time I was already ready to risk it all. "I'm free Friday," I said, as I caught him looking at my breasts, then he pulled his phone out and put my number in. "So if I call, your mans not gonna answer and trip is he?" he said with a smirk. "I'm single and if I wasn't I wouldn't have given you my number," I told him. "People don't value relationships anymore so I have to ask," he offered. I caught a slight look of disappointment in his eyes that quickly went away. "Well, I gotta get going." It was hot as hell and I was starting to sweat. "It was nice meeting you," I said, as I walked past him towards my car. "Nice meeting you too, I'll hit you soon," he said, as he looked me over from head to toe and smiled with approval. He walked away and I got into my car and did a dance. I was excited I met someone.

Although me and Drew broke up a couple weeks ago, our relationship had been over the last three months. In my head Drew had potential and that was the problem, it stayed in my head and never became a reality. When we first met, I knew he had issues. But the nurturer in me wanted to help, fix, and mold him into the man he said he wanted to be and the man I knew he could be. And in the midst of everything I fell in love with him. I fell in love with how perfect we could have been, but he strung me along and used me for all I had with no intentions of doing better. People like that gave you just enough hope within the relationship to make you stay. As hard as it was to pull myself out the grave I had dug for myself, I found the strength to do so. I had had it with the cheating, broken promises, and the street life. How the hell did I get caught with a thug? The same way most good girls do. He was fine, he could fuck, and he was a master manipulator that was a pro at gaslighting. He knew exactly how to play on my emotions. Men like that were raised on survival and not love. Whether it was surviving from the streets or surviving in prison, it is all they know, and love sometimes isn't shown or received properly. I would be lying if I said I didn't love him anymore, I just made the decision to love myself more. One thing for sure I wanted to know more about Blu, there was just something about him and I couldn't wait to taste.... I mean get to know him.

CHAPTER 3

It's Monday so that means getting to the money. I rented a small office space in Oakdale Office Park. It had a small waiting area, a small office, and a room for me and my clients for our therapy sessions. I was with a client that was fairly new, he had been coming weekly for the last three weeks. Mr. Johnson was an older black man in his late 50s. He was a small quiet guy, but very sweet, and was always trying to flirt. He was cute in a 'I wanna pinch grandpa's cheeks' kind of way. I would have to keep reverting the conversation back to him because I wasn't sure if he was flirting or if it was early signs of dementia. Mr. Johnson was sitting on the couch while I sat in a chair facing him. He said " Why are you not married, your boyfriend better hurry up before a 'lil old man like me getcha." I laughed and said, " I'm single and have no plans of getting married soon, but tell me about some of the important relationships you have in your life." Then my client went on to talk about his past relationships. As he was talking my mind started to wander off thinking about Blu. I wondered what he looked like with his shirt off. I was a sucka for a guy with some nice arms and chest. My man gotta be able to pick me up and throw me across the room WWE style. I accidently let out a small laugh, laughing at myself. Mr. Johnson said, "I'm sorry did you say something?" I said, "Oh no, I was just clearing my throat, please continue." Ten minutes later our session was over and he rebooked for the next Monday. I was happy he was my last client of the day because I couldn't wait to get home and call Jessica and tell her about my mystery guy.

On the way home I stopped by the 7-Eleven and got a bottle of wine. I left there to go pick up a pizza from All American Pizza on Macarthur, one of my fav pizza spots. I pulled into my garage at my three bedroom, two bath house. Once inside, I set my stuff on the counter and pulled off all of my clothes and got in the shower. After my shower, I threw on some panties and an oversized T-shirt, grabbed my favorite blanket and headed for the couch, stopping to get my pizza and wine. I ate the pizza out of the box and drank my wine straight out of the bottle. Before opening my bottle I decided to take a picture of my wine, Stella Rosa Berry, for Snap. Now that I was comfortable on the couch and watching `The Office´ on Netflix, I called my bestie. As soon as she said hello I yelled, "Jessica!" She laughed, "Girl what?" "I met this baddie yesterday and girlllll he's thicker than molasses!" She burst out laughing "Girl shut up." I'm excited at this point not that it takes much for me to get excited. I kept talking, "Girl he be in the GYM gym, he got a cute butt too and you know I was looking. We both laughed for a cool minute and were being goofy. I told Jessica about how I ran into him. She said, "So his real name is Blu." "I don't know, I think so." Then she said, "Girl you gotta verify the name so you can look him up on social media. He could have a whole family he's hiding or see if he's in the system and make sure he ain't crazy." I said, "Well damn, let me make it to the first date and get some more info." "Ok girl just be careful. People be weird and be snakes hiding in plain sight." I thought about what she said for a second. "Hello?" "Yeah I hear you, I'll be careful." Jessica asked if I heard from Lexi and filled me in on her latest scandal. "Yeah, Lexi must had hit the jackpot with her latest scheme, she's been shopping and eating good. You haven't been seeing her Snaps and Instagram stories?" "Damn, for real, and no I haven't been on Snap much and I didn't see her story on Instagram. I was talking to her yesterday and she mentioned she was gonna plan to take a trip to Miami." Jessica was shook "Miamiiii? How the hell she can afford that and I can barely afford to take a nap?" "I thought she was just talking, I didn't know she had come up on some money." I could literally feel Jessica rolling her eyes through the phone. "Well you know she will go through that money quick like she always do and be asking us to borrow money that she will never pay back." Jessica stated with annoyance. I sighed, "I don't understand why she won't at least stack her paper and put it towards a business or something or go to school." "She pushing 30 so she need to do something with her life." "Maybe we should talk to her," I suggested. Jessica corrected me, "Aht aht YOU should talk to her, that's your friend." Not really surprised by her comment "Don't be like that," I sighed. "Nah I tolerate Lexi cause of you, but you know you can't trust females like that, they will sell you out for two dollars and a happy meal." "OMG she is not that bad." Jessica laughed and continued "I mean she cool, but I keep her at a distance because I don't want to get caught up in any mess." "I understand for real but she wouldn't do anything that low." I decided to change the subject. We talked for another 30 minutes about celebrity gossip and personal goals that we had for ourselves that we were trying to meet. Jessica talked about how close she was to getting her dream home and the life she wanted to provide for Anya and herself.

After I got off the phone I got ready for work the next day, then got in the bed. I had to admit I was a little disappointed I hadn't heard from Blu. I told myself to relax, he will call. I closed my eyes and tried to go to sleep, but my brain wouldn't let me. I started thinking about my life and everything I had been through with Drew. If I was being completely honest with myself I wasn't completely over him. I know it is going to take some time, but I was hoping that Blu could help me to not think about him so much and at the same time I didn't want to treat him like a rebound. Eventually, I fell asleep.

Chapter 4

I woke up in a panic because I hadn't heard my alarm go off. I grabbed my phone to check time and it was 6:55 AM, five minutes before my alarm was due to go off. As my eyes adjusted to the light coming from my phone I noticed I had a text message from an unknown number. It read:

Unknown number: Good morning

I'm far from a morning person but that made me chipper up. It had to be Blu, he had sent it ten minutes ago. I sat up in bed and started typing:

Bre: Good morning handsome.

I threw the handsome in there for the razzle dazzle. I got up and stretched and drank a bottle of water. I had read that it was good to drink a bottle of water when you wake up to help rid your body of toxins your body works hard to remove throughout the night while you sleep. I wasn't a health nut, nor was I always in the gym, but I tried to be a little bit healthy by making those small changes and adding veggies and fruit in my diet. I wasn't skinny by any means, I was curvy and I wasn't talking about Instagram/video model curvy but the type of curves that came with a little stomach and thighs to match. Although I could stand to lose 10 to 15 pounds, I have learned to love my body and the family genes that blessed me with my ass and double D's that people pay big money for.

I got up, brushed my teeth, washed my face, and laid my edges. I checked my phone.

Unknown number: How are you this morning? This is Blu btw.

Bre: I'm doing good, ready to get this day started. How bout u?

I saved his number and started getting dressed. As I was pulling my braids up into a bun, I heard a notification from my phone.

Blu: I can't complain but I was wanting to see if you are still free Friday, maybe we can go to one of your favorite spots.

A smile came across my face and I said out loud "hell yeah," then I dropped down and got my eagle on.

Bre: Friday works good for me, I'm free after 5:30.

My last client was at 2:00 PM on Friday, but I wanted to make sure I had time to get my shit together. I needed to get my outfit together, figure out how I was going to wear my hair, my makeup, and of course I needed time to talk to Jessica so she could hype me up. I hadn't been on a date in years, probably since... I immediately stopped my thoughts and pushed Drew out my head. He was the last person I wanted to think about. I now had something to look forward to.

CHAPTER 5

It was Thursday and I was having lunch with my girls at Chili's on Memorial. I'm at the table happy to be eating, I love food, and I didn't miss any meals. We shared a spinach dip as we waited for our entrée and we each had a drink in front of us. Lexi's ass was high and giggling at everything and she was eating all the damn chips. Jessica was scrolling through Instagram and I was drinking and running my mouth. "Y'all I am so nervous about this date tomorrow." I had heard from Blu once since we texted Tuesday morning but it was small talk through text. I continued rambling, "What if the conversation is trash and it's all awkward or what if I mess my words up like I do when I'm excited." Jessica looked up from her phone, "Like the time you said cosmopolitan ice cream instead of neapolitan ice cream?" Lexi choked on her chip laughing. I rolled my eyes, "Uh yeah I didn't need an example." Jessica laughed, "Bre relax, I'm sure you will keep the conversation going with all the questions you be asking." Lexi added, "Yeah you do be giving people the third degree." Lexi had on a lace front wig that looked no cheaper than $500 and not to mention the stiletto nails with jewels on every finger. She caught me checking out her nails and said, "You like?" She did the damn spirit fingers all in my face. "Yeah I see you with the drip around your wrist too. You back stripping?" I joked. "Uh un I was not a stripper, I just danced at a couple parties and dassit," she said as she tried to make her voice sound like Ebony from the movie, 'The Players Club.' Jessica gave a yeah right look that Lexi didn't catch. Lexi added "But nah this new dude I'm talking to keep your girl right." Jessica looked at Lexi

"Who?" "Don't worry about it, you don't know him." Lexi snapped back. Jessica snapped back also, "I mean OKC ain't that big so I probably do." Me and Jessica both stared at Lexi waiting for a response and it was obvious she wasn't going to say. I tried to lighten the mood, "Ooookay, well it seems like you having fun, just try not to get caught up in any drama." Lexi was scrolling through her phone acting like she was ignoring us. Jessica decided to be petty, "And maybe you should start saving your money instead of splurging on material things." I gave her a 'why did you go there' stare. Lexi gave Jessica a death stare. I looked at Lexi and I tried to be softer than how Jessica just said it, "Lexi she right we been worried about you and we your friends we just trying to look out for you." I didn't want to have the conversation like this, but I definitely wouldn't be a good friend if I didn't care enough to say something. My practice was doing well and Jessica was doing the damn thing so I felt like Lexi should try to level up. Lexi put her phone down and even though me and Jessica both brought it up she stared and spoke directly to me, "Bre stop trying to be my mama, Imma a grown ass woman and I can take care of myself. I don't need your advice. I just choose not to live a boring ass life like you two." She glanced at Jessica. Jessica blurted, "I'll take my boring ass life over all the illegal ratchet ass shit you do. You gonna end up dead or locked up." I added "And I'm not trying to be your mom, just trying to make sure you good." I suddenly wished this subject hadn't had come up. Lexi stood up and started grabbing her things, "I'm leaving, y'all being annoying as fuck right now." As Lexi was leaving the table Jessica yelled "Hold up, you ate half these chips and you ain't paid for your drink!" Lexi was at the door by now with her middle finger in the air. Jessica looked at me, "See, bitches be disrespectful." "You looking at me like it's my fault," I said, feeling guilty. "Just getcho friend. She being weird." I sighed, "Yeah that was childish." Not sure where her sudden outburst came from but I was going to text her later.

Me and Jessica finished our drinks and the waiter brought our food. We didn't let how Lexi acted ruin our lunch. We laughed and talked about random shit and she updated me on mom life. The love in her face when she talked about her daughter Anya was so apparent. "Girl she is so smart and sassy like me, it's scary." I laughed remembering when I had visited them last week and she provided us with all the entertainment we needed. Jessica asked, "So what's the plan for your big date tomorrow?" "We are going to my favorite Vietnamese pho spot and keep it casual." Jessica nodded, "That sounds cool. Have you seen or talked to Drew since y'all broke up?" "Nah his pride and guilty conscience won't allow him to and I'm definitely not going to and I'm sure he got him a new girl by now." Jessica got serious, "You been doing ok with the breakup?" "I'm doing ok, it's getting a little easier as time passes and I have been keeping busy to keep my mind off things." "Ok, well you know I am here if you need me and if you need me to pull up on him and pop the trunk." Jessica put her hands up like she was holding a gun and started making gun noises. I could always count on Jessica to make me laugh and I know she low key meant what she said. Lexi would probably say we were some "squares" or "good girls" but me and Jess may not go looking for trouble, but we for damn sure will finish it.

CHAPTER 6

Girl the way you movin'
Got me in a trance, DJ turn me up
Ladies dis yo Jam, Imma sip Moscato
And you gone lose dem pants
Then Imma throw this money while you do it with no hands
Girlll drop it to the floorrrr, I love the way yo booty goooooo....
(No Hands by Waka Flaka)

I was in my room, in the mirror dancing, listening to some music. It was 5:00 PM, Friday, and I was meeting Blu in an hour at PHO 54 on North May Ave. It was a small family owned Vietnamese restaurant, but had good food, and it was something different he said he hadn't had before. We had spoken earlier to confirm the place and time. I stood in my walk-in closet trying to decide what to wear. I decided on some olive green cargo type shorts and tan v-neck shirt. I paired the outfit with some chocolate strappy sandals. I added some big gold hoop earrings and my favorite gold "B" necklace. I put on liner, mascara, and my gloss bomb lip gloss. And I finished with leaving my braids down with the front pinned back. As I was finishing getting dressed I thought about the day we met in the parking lot. He was so handsome and had such a sexy voice. I was a little concerned that we had not talked much since we met on Sunday, but I figured it is better to get to know each other face to face. I just hope he had a good personality.

I texted Blu to let him know I was heading to the restaurant. I smiled and my nerves started to take over. I grabbed my purse and mask and headed out the door. Blu texted back said he was almost there. As I drove I thought about my life. I have always stressed about the future and never enjoyed the now. Although I wanted to get married and have a family someday, I also didn't want to rush or force anything. I had come from a broken family and I did not want to repeat the cycle. But for now, I am going to take some risk and have some fun.

I pulled into the parking lot right in front of the restaurant. I text:

Bre: I'm here

Blu: I'm inside to the right in a booth

I looked through the window of the restaurant to see if I could see him. It made me anxious he was going to watch me get out of the car and walk in. My stomach started hurting and my mouth was dry as cotton, but I sucked it up and got out of the car and headed in. Once inside it took just a second to spot him. He smiled and stood up. As soon as I saw him my nerves went out the window and I suddenly felt relaxed and comfortable. He was fine, just like I remembered. He was dressed in jeans with red and blue Js and a red and white shirt. I walked over to him and hugged him, "It's nice to see you again." A little caught off guard at first, he hugged me back, "Good to see you too." I'm not sure what cologne he was wearing, but it smelled so damn good I just wanted to bury my nose in his neck and smell him all day. His chest and arms felt like my bed, a bed that I needed to lay in every night.

We sat down and the waiter took our drinks. "You look beautiful." I smiled "Thank you." We looked over the menu and had small talk. I recommended steak and brisket pho and I ordered the same with spring rolls as an appetizer. The waiter left and put our orders in. Blu asked what I did for a living and I told him. "So what do you do for a living?" I asked. "I'm a truck driver, been one going on eight years." "Oh ok, you must don't mind being on the road all the time." "No, it's not too bad, I'm used to it, keeps the bills paid." We did the usual first date conversation. Where you from? Kids? Marriage? Those types of questions. He has a five year old son, never been married, and born and raised in OKC. We exchanged funny stories of our lives and partying in our 20's. We had conversations about family, goals, and hobbies. We talked about everything. He was so smooth and charming and kept me laughing and I loved a guy that could make me laugh and a guy I could be goofy with. We were vibing well together and I could tell he was enjoying himself also. As we ate the conversation got a little deeper and the topic of past relationships came up. He took a bite of his pho and asked, "So what happened between you and your ex?" "He didn't want to step up. I needed him to be a man, be respectful, and want better for himself and I guess he either didn't want to do that with me or he didn't want to do it at all. And when someone shows you who they are you have to believe them even though it took my dumbass almost 3 years to realize that." He nodded his head as if he completely understood. He asked, "What did he do for a living?" His question caught me off guard and I was also a little embarrassed to admit that my ex was a big time drug dealer and he had been in the game since he was a kid. When we first started dating I had no intentions on getting serious, but I ended up falling for him. Realizing being with someone like that could hurt my career, I tried to persuade and push him to get out the game and go legit. At first he seemed for it, but he ended up leading me on a journey of lies and manipulation. He had no intentions of changing and he knew from the beginning but he couldn't let me go. Blu stared at me waiting for an answer. "He was an entrepreneur." That was kind of the truth. He asked "You two still communicate?" "It's been a couple weeks since we spoke but enough about him." I didn't want to talk about him anymore, the more he was on my mind the more I thought about what he was doing and who he was with. "I'm sorry, I didn't mean to be in your business, but you can tell a lot about a person from their past relationship." I thought about the saying 'you are who you lay with' and he was right. I was mad at myself for giving him the time of day and even more mad that I loved him the way I did. So much time wasted. How could I forgive myself? I had zoned out, I had a million thoughts in my head. "Bre, are you ok?" "Yes I'm fine, I was just thinking about what you said and yes you can tell some things about a person based off their past, but sometimes people make mistakes and sometimes people just try to see the good in others and become blinded by love." He gave me an applause and said "Preach! I have been there before." I laughed at him being extra. He continued "I bet you are really good at what you do." "I try," I said with a smile. It was my turn to ask some questions, "So what happened in your last relationship?" "Not much to tell, we didn't work out and now we just concentrate on co-parenting." With an eyebrow raised I said "Nah bro you was just in my business a second ago so Imma need more than that." He laughed "We just wasn't compatible." His answers were short, but I didn't want to seem bothered or aggressive so I let it go for now. I changed the subject "So do you have a Snap or an Instagram?" "No, I don't do social media, it is too much drama and unnecessary stress and pressure." "That's something I don't see often." "What?" "You don't often see people our age that don't have any social media." "It just doesn't interest me." "So is Blu short for something?" He smiled, "Blu is the name my mother gave me, why you want to look me up and see if I am lying?" Yes. "No." He stared at me and then I said, "Sooooo, what you say your last name was again?" He laughed knowing that would be my next question. "My name is Blu Wilson." I decided to pull my phone out of my purse and search his name, right there in front of him. He sat quietly and watched me. He had a smile on his face as if he was impressed with my boldness. I searched his name on Instagram, Facebook, Twitter and Snapchat and did not find him. I put my phone up and he asked, "You have trust issues?" "Who doesn't?" I wanted to ask for his ID, because for some reason I wasn't satisfied, but I knew that would be doing too much. I had just met this man and already had assumed he was lying about his name. Damn my ex did a number on me.

We finished our food about 40 minutes ago, but we were still talking and enjoying each other's company. The attraction was real and we had a lot in common. He was telling me about a funny story that had happened at work. My mind wandered off. My mind went to his lips, then his shoulders and chest. I wondered to myself how long should I wait before I invite him over one time for the one time. I was so deep in my imagination I had reached across the table and grabbed his bicep. Shocked, he laughed and gave me this sexy look. "I'm sorry I just been admiring your body, looks like you live in the gym." "The gym my second home, I gotta keep my weight and strength up. I like thick women, I gotta be able to pick you... I mean pick them up." Shiddddd this motha fucka spitting that hot fire. All I could do was clench my imaginary pearls, lean back and in a high pitch voice say "Okaay." He laughed and winked at me and I melted on the inside.

As he paid for the bill he told me how he enjoyed the food. We headed to the exit and he held the door open for me as we walked outside. "I'm right here," I said as I pointed to my car. This was the part I wasn't looking forward to, that awkwardness of where you are at the end of the date where you decide if you are going to kiss or not. I had pretty much felt the man up so I might as well kiss him. "I want to choose the next spot," he said as he stepped closer to me. "Sounds good to me." I was excited to know he wanted to see me again. At this point my car door is open and we are standing close. He leaned in and hugged me and gave me a squeeze. In my ear he said, "I'll call you later." He released his hold and as he pulled back he kissed me. At first it was a peck on the lips, then he leaned in for a second kiss. I felt my body shiver. I started to slowly open my mouth, but he pulled away. He winked at me and said, "See you later." I got in my car and he closed the door for me and headed towards his car. Where did this man come from? I laid my head on the headrest and took in a deep breath. I started my car and pulled out of the parking spot and looked to see what car he was in, but he was gone.

CHAPTER 7

I got home after my date and decided to soak in the tub with a glass of wine. I thought about Blu and how his lips felt and how my body felt good in his arms. I picked up my phone and called Jessica. She didn't answer. I'm sure Anya was keeping her busy. Then I thought about Lexi. I hadn't talked to her since her outburst yesterday at Chili's. I called her and she answered on the first ring, "Hey shawty what it do." She said in her T pain voice. I laughed. She continued "I was just thinking about you." "Oh you wanted to yell at me some more?" "Bre, I know you just looking out for me, but I'm going to live my life the way I want." I rolled my eyes, but she was right. I'm just going to mind my business. "Ok, e ok live your life booboo." "Thank you. Sooo you want to go out with me tomorrow?" "Wow, two weekends in a row, you trying to turn me out or something?" I joked. "Come on, we had fun last weekend." She begged. I remembered how I wanted to enjoy life and have more fun, so I agreed. She yelled "Ayyye turn up!" I thought about Jessica, "Hopefully Jessica can get a babysitter on such a short notice." "How about just me and you go. You know Jessica don't like me and honestly the feeling is mutual." "Now you know I'm not about to NOT invite Jessica and like you said we ALL had a good time, so chill." Lexi let out a big sigh "Whatever." I told Lexi about how my date went. "Yayyy girl I am excited for you. You deserve to have some fun and now you got you some business and you can stay out of mine." She laughed and I had to admit it was funny I laughed too, "Hold up now, I do got business AND a business." I joked back. "But yes I do deserve this." I smiled. Lexi started talking about planning a trip to Vegas. I made sure I just listened and didn't ask too many questions, I didn't want her to think I was in her business. Then I heard what sounded like a knock on Lexi's door. "Girl I gotta go, babe is here." You could tell she was excited, she hung up before I could say bye. This guy had her sprung.

I added some more hot water in my tub and laid back. I thought about Blu. Either he put some type of spell on me or I was just lonely. I thought about his comment about picking me up and laughed to myself. The wine had me feeling good and my body was relaxed after soaking in the hot water. I closed my eyes and thought about what it would be like to be with Blu. I decided to explore my body, something I hadn't done in a while. I thought about us both naked. I imagined him exploring my body with his hands first, then with his tongue. I cupped my breast. In my mind it was him doing it. I massaged them. One hand was on my breast and the other traveled downward. I spread open my lips and found my clit. I applied slight pressure while moving my hand in a circular motion. Then I found the spot I had familiarized myself with, a spot I discovered in my late teens. I applied a little bit more pressure and moved my hands a little faster. My body started to heat up. I started breathing hard. I kept going. Then my body stiffened and my much needed orgasm came. I let out a loud moan. My breathing lessened and slowly my body started to relax. I laid in the tub a little longer, then I got out and dried off. I put on some comfy clothes and got in the bed. As I was browsing Netflix, my phone rang. I checked to see who was calling and it was Jessica. I answered and yelled "Giirrrllllllll!"

CHAPTER 8

The next morning I met Jessica and Anya for breakfast. Anya picked the spot so we were at Waffle House on Memorial. As we were waiting for our food, Anya was talking a mile a minute. She was telling us about school, the new Tik Tok dances and what she wanted to do for her upcoming birthday in September. The server brought our food out and we started eating. Jessica asked, "Have you heard from Blu?" "No I haven't, you think I should call or text him?" "No, I'm sure he will call, relax." "I am relaxed, why you always telling me to relax, I'm chilling." I said a little louder than I intended. Jessica laughed, "Yeah you sound relaxed to me." I laughed at myself, "Yeah I am a little turnt." Anya threw in her two cents "Mmmm hmmm." I looked at Anya and laughed. She was getting older and I realized I had better be careful with what I say around her. So I said, "So Anya, what should I do?" Without hesitation "He will call you cause you kinda cute." Me and Jessica laughed. "Well thank you Anya." Jessica looked at her daughter and sighed, "Girl you are getting too grown." Anya realized that was her cue to finish eating so she took a bite of her eggs. "So me and Lexi going out tonight, you want to join us?" Jessica looked at me liked I asked her a stupid question, "After the way she acted at the restaurant, Imma give that a strong hell no." "Really Jess, y'all have argued way worse before and made up so why not just come hang with us? We had fun last time, right?" "It was your birthday and you know I wasn't going to miss that, but I just don't want to be bothered with her and her shenanigans." I threw my hands up, "Ok I give up trying to be the peacemaker." She took a bite of her waffle and whispered, "Thank you." She continued "So where y'all going?"

"Probably to Pink in Bricktown." "Well have fun." She said sarcastically. Before I could respond my phone went off, it was a text from Blu. I started cheesing. Anya said, "That's your boyfriend ain't it?" I replied "You are just too much." I reached over and pinched her cheeks. Then I looked back at my phone and stared at it. Jessica interrupted my thoughts "Hellloooo, what does it say?" "It say 'wyd'". "I know you is not over there cheesing over a 'wyd' text," she laughed. Anya with the two cents "OOooo girl he like you." "Anya finish your food." Jessica snapped and gave her that universal mom look of death. "So what you going to say back?" Hearing Jessica be excited for me reminded me of the times in high school when we used to coach each other on what to say to guys over the phone or through texts. "I'm just going to say me and my day uno outchea in these streets grinding." I said as I was bouncing my shoulders hyping all of us up. Jessica burst out laughing "Stawwpppp playing with me, witcho goofy ass." I started typing my text "I'm just going to say out with the bestie having brunch. Ya know, keep it real cute and simple." Jessica shook her head and slapped her palm on her forehead and I just laughed. She was so over my extra ass, but I just smiled at her because I know she loves me. I hit send and started twerking in my seat with my tongue out. "OMG girl you already whipped after the first date." I rolled my eyes "No I'm not." I lied. Anya was smiling as if she knew I was lying too.

We paid for our food and I hugged Anya and Jessica and we said our goodbyes. As I got in the car Blu texted back:

Blu: When can I see you again?
Bre: I have plans tonight. You want to do brunch or dinner tomorrow?

I hit send and pulled out the parking lot. When I got home I went through my closet to find something to wear for tonight. He texted back:

Blu: That sounds good to me. I'll pick the spot this time. You made it home yet?

Bre: yes

Next thing I know he was calling me, I instantly got nervous, but excited to hear his voice. I answered and played it smooth as much as I could. He seemed excited to hear from me also. It was so relaxing to talk to him. We ended up talking on the phone for almost two hours. I hadn't talked like that in a long time and I enjoyed every bit of it. I loved his personality. We both couldn't wait to see each other tomorrow. We had so much chemistry and there was some sexual tension. We got off the phone and I took a nap so I could be ready for tonight.

CHAPTER 9

I was in the bathroom listening to some Beyonce.

I may be young but I'm ready, to give you all my loveee
I told my girls you can get it, don't slow it down just let it goo
So in loveeee, I'll give it all away. Just don't tell nobody tomorrow.....
(Party by Beyonce')

I was finishing up my makeup. I decided to wear a black fitted dress that stopped mid thigh with some thigh high red boots that had criss cross straps on the back that went up the leg. I called Lexi to confirm if we were going to Pink. Lexi answered, "Hey girl you ready to turn up tonight?" I heard music in the background and you could tell she was smoking. Lexi was always smoking and Jessica was a smoker too. That was one thing that brought them together because I rarely did. I was more of a drinker. I enjoyed wine when I was home chilling and I did shots of brown when I decided to go out. "Yep I'm ready. What you wearing?" Lexi said she was wearing some leather like leggings and a crop top and some pumps. "That sounds cute, so where are we going tonight?" "You know I want to go to Pink." Which I was cool with, it was a cool spot so I said, "Ok cool what time you want to meet down there?" I always drove and mostly by myself and met everyone there because I was the type that when I was ready to go, I was ready to go. There had been a few times I left Jessica, Lexi, and other friends at the club. I never left a friend alone though and I never let a friend leave drunk with a guy they didn't know. Lexi answered, "Let's get there by 11." I reminded Lexi that I wasn't about to be out all damn night and she agreed and said she had something to do Sunday. Curious, I asked, "What you gotta do Sunday?" "Aht Aht you in my business." A little offended that my friend was being so secretive lately I said, "Damn girl I was just curious. No need to do me like that, we friends ain't we?" She did a loud sigh, "Yes, you know we are. Text me when you leaving the house ok?" "Ok." And she hung up. I wanted to call her back, because I didn't like how she rushed me off the phone like that, but I was in a good mood and feeling cute so I let it go.

It was 10:40 PM and I was putting on my boots. I sent a text to Lexi letting her know I was leaving. I decided to take a quick selfie showing off my outfit and posted it on my Instagram. Feeling cute I decided to send the picture I took to Blu since he wasn't on social media. I grabbed my keys and headed to the car. As I pulled out of the driveway I looked at my phone and I had two messages.

Lexi: ok

Blu: You look sexy.

Blu text had me smiling. I texted back.

Bre: Thank you ☺

I hopped on the turnpike and headed downtown playing my music loud. Music was my therapy. When you can't find the words you want to say, they were in music and when your anxiety was on a level ten, music was there to drown out your thoughts. Music took my imagination and thoughts to another place. There was music for every mood. And my mood right now was me feeling good about myself and where I was in life. I left my toxic ex, I was out enjoying myself, and I was dating. And not to mention I was doing well in my career.

You got a hunnid bands, you got a baby benz
You got some bad friends. High school pics, you was even bad then
You ain't stressin off no lover in the past tense
You already had them.
Work at 8 A.M. finish 'round 5...

(Nice For What by Drake)

I got to Bricktown in downtown OKC and it was quite a few people out. As I was searching for a parking spot, it reminded me of why I try to avoid downtown. It was hard to find good parking, either you had to park far away or pay too much for a spot. I found a spot in a lot in walking distance from Pink. I checked my phone, but no messages from Lexi. So I texted her and told her I was here and where I had parked. I sat in my car scrolling through social media as I waited. I scrolled through Instagram, Snapchat, and Facebook and after laughing at a couple memes, I still hadn't heard from Lexi. What the hell is she doing? Ten minutes had gone by so I dialed her number. It rang several times and went to voicemail. I waited another five minutes. At this point any type of good vibe I was feeling was gone. I tried calling her again and still no answer. She was probably high. I decided to wait a little longer. It had now been 30 minutes and I was fuming. I could have stayed home and been in my bed watching TV I know Lexi could be a little selfish at times, but she done fucked up and I was going to cuss her smooth out the next time I saw her. I threw my phone in the passenger seat and as soon as I put my car in reverse there was a knock on my driver side window. I screamed a scream that you only hear in movies, so loud I'm sure the people in the hotel across the street heard me. I looked to see who it was hoping I wasn't about to get robbed. It was Blu. I rolled down my window. "You scared the shit out of me! What the hell are you doing here?" Blu couldn't help but laugh at the way I screamed, "My bad, I didn't mean

36

to scare you, I was just leaving from hanging out with my friends. Why are you leaving, I thought you were going out." "Lexi's ass stood me up and not answering my calls." "Damn that's messed up and you all dressed up." "I know," I said disappointed. "If you want we can go somewhere. Drinks are on me." He smiled and showed his dimple, his smile could calm a war down. "Sure." I grabbed my stuff and got out of the car. "You parked over here?" I asked. "Yeah, over there." He pointed. I looked in the direction he pointed "Which one?" Before he could answer, my phone rang. It was Lexi. I hit the talk button and immediately went off. "Why the fuck would you ask me to come out with you and you don't show or answer the damn phone. It's 11:45, what the hell was you doing?" Lexi immediately started apologizing. "Bre, I'm so sorry. I got into it with my boyfriend and he took my phone and started going through it and found some stuff and started acting crazy but I'm on my way now." "You might as well turn around because I'm not in the mood nor am I waiting in any lines." Lexi pleaded, "I'm like 15 minutes away, we can still do something." I was over it and honestly at the moment I rather hang out with Blu, "Nah I'm good." Lexi now had an attitude, "It's not even that serious but whatever." "How the fuck you gone be mad at me when you had me sitting..." Click. I looked at my phone and she had hung up. I looked at my phone, "Oh hell no!" Blu's mouth was open, hell he was shocked too, she had the audacity. I looked at him, "How SHE mad?" Blu laughed "You got a mouth piece on you, it's cute though." He grabbed me and kissed me and said, "I've been wanting to do that all day." I smiled, "Is that why you stalking me?" He laughed. I continued, "I been thinking about our kiss all day too." He smiled and stared into my eyes as if he wanted to say something so I said, "You sure you don't mind hanging out with me?" "Not at all, I'd be happy to. I enjoy your company." "Ok cool, where you want to go?" "Wellll, I remember you said you love to dance soooooo..." He looked at me and smiled while rubbing his hands together. I was feeling a little shy about him seeing me dance. He sensed it, "Oh you scared?" "No, it's just almost 12:00 AM and the clubs are packed and probably not letting anyone in." He rubbed his beard, "You must not know this my city." I looked at him with my face twisted up like boyyy you ain't nobody. I joked, "You act like you play for OKC Thunder or something." He smacked his lips together, "What's my name?" I just looked at him and laughed. Like are you serious? He said, "You can either say it now or scream it later, your choice?" My knees buckled just a lil bit. I played it cool and started walking, "I think you got too much dip on your chip sir." He burst out laughing and walked with me.

We got to Pink and it was packed, but surprisingly the line wasn't too long. Blu grabbed my hand and we walked to the front of the line. The bouncer saw us and he dapped and hugged Blu and we walked right in. Blu looked at me and winked. Impressed, I gave a nod of approval. Who the hell does he think he is? We went straight to the bar and he bought us two shots of Crown each. After we took them, I checked out the scene. People were either at the tables vibing and having a good time or on the dance floor turning up. Pink was a smaller club, but the music was always good. The DJ played Pop That by French Montana and the secret inner stripper in me came out. I grabbed Blu and pulled him to the dance floor. There was a spot by the wall on the dance floor, so I guided him there. The dance floor got packed and people were dancing in the aisle and at their tables. I had bent over in front of Blu and was giving him the business. And to my surprise he was keeping up. I heard him yell, "That thang thangginnn!" That hyped me up even more. We were in sync. The chemistry between us was undeniable. Two more songs had played and we were still dancing. His hands started to explore my body. I could tell he was turned on and he wanted me. The DJ switched it up and played some slow jams.

I...lose... all control.
When... you... grab a hold
And... you... do your trick
I... love... it when you
Lickkkkk.....

(Lick by Joi)

We were now face to face, holding each other, my arms around his neck and his arms around my waist. He put his head in the crease of my neck and I could feel his lips graze my neck. I felt throbbing in between my legs. I was so turned on. He whispered in my ear, "Is it too soon to take you home with me tonight?" A small part of me said it was too soon, but a big part of me wanted him now. When I didn't answer right away he pulled back and looked at me, "Hope I'm not coming off as aggressive, it's no pressure. I'll follow your lead." I said, "No, it's ok, I want to but I do want you to know I like you a lot and want to get to know you more and that I don't want it to be just sex." Blu said, "I won't ghost you if that's what you're worried about. I want to get to know you more too." I smiled. I don't know who his mama is but her son was about to get ALL of this. He leaned in and kissed me passionately and my body felt on fire. He grabbed my hand and guided me to the exit. I felt like I was floating and everything was in slow motion. Like in the movies. I'm about to ride him 'til the wheels fall off.

CHAPTER 10

He walked me to my car. We were both smiling like some kids. I started up my car and watched him go get in his. He pulled out the parking lot and I was right behind him. He drove a new black BMW, it was really nice. My adrenaline was pumping and I was excited. I needed a song to hype me up. I scrolled through my phone, found a song and I turned that shit up.

Just a lil ten piece for her
Just to blow it in the mall, doesn't mean we're involved
I just what, I just uh
Put a Richard on the card
I ain't grow up playing ball
But I'll show you.. how the fuck.. you gotta do it....
                    (Going Bad by Drake and Meek Mill)

My hand was in the air and I was yelling and rapping alone like I wrote the lyrics. Nothing like rapping the lyrics straight through and not messing up. They should've had me in the video. I laughed at myself. I had a slight buzz and was feeling good about my decision to follow Blu to his place. We pulled into some apartments off of Macarthur. My stomach started doing flips. Relax. I took a deep breath. We got to his building and I pulled into the parking spot beside him. We got out at the same time. He walked over to me and grabbed my hand and led the way like he did at the club. I felt relaxed and safe. He looked at me as he opened the door and smiled and said, "I'm still in the process of moving so most of my furniture I ordered isn't here yet." "You have a bed?" I don't care how fine he was, I wasn't doing it on the floor... Nah I'm lying I probably would. We would have been rolling around all over this floor. He smiled, "Yes." In his apartment it was empty. No furniture, no TV, and no home décor. "How long have you been here?" I asked. "A little over a week, I'm hoping most of my stuff will be here on Monday." "Oh ok." I continued to look around. It was a small two bedroom, one bath. As if he read my mind he said, "I'm stacking my money to buy a house for me and my son, so I'm cutting corners where needed." "Makes sense." I walked to his bedroom and he followed me. In his room there was a queen size bed that was made up with lots of pillows and a blanket folded on top of the comforter. On the floor there was some boxes and a plasma TV sitting on top of them. He turned on some music on his phone and asked if I wanted a drink. "No thank you." "Get comfortable," He said. Even though his place didn't have the at home feel, I felt comfortable. I took my boots off and as I was about to sit on the bed. He grabbed me and pulled me close. His shirt was off. When the hell did he do that? My hands rubbed his arms and chest. Then I rubbed his soft beard. "When did you sneak your shirt off?" He smiled, "While you were taking off your boots." I started unbuckling his belt and undid his pants. He just stared at me while I did it. He grabbed my hands as if to stop me. "You change your mind?" I asked hoping he didn't. He smiled and shook his head. He grabbed my face and kissed me. He held me tight. I slid my hand down his pants anxious to see what he was working with. Jackpot. He was perfect in length and thickness and he was hard as a rock. His hands went under my dress and he lifted it over my head and threw it on the floor. He popped my bra straps, took my bra off, and threw it on the floor. I pulled my panties off and he pulled his jeans and underwear off. He laid me back on the bed. He took his hands and cupped them behind my knees and pushed my knees towards my chest. He got on his knees on the floor and he used his tongue to part open my lips. I was not

41

expecting this at all and if he would have seen my face, he would have seen my mouth wide open. He licked around my clit, teasing me, then he finally licked right on it. I let out a moan. I was anticipating his next move. He applied gentle pressure with his tongue and alternated up and down in circular motions on and around my clit. I arched my back and grabbed a handful of the sheets to try to contain myself. After every few licks he kissed my clit softly. I wanted to scream. I couldn't believe he was making me feel this way. He released one of my legs and inserted two fingers and started gently moving them in and out and his tongue didn't miss a beat. I was shooketh. Not only was I not expecting him to go down on me, but I was not expecting him to be good at it. So many guys think they are good at oral but are terrible at it. But Blu he listened and paid attention to my body language knowing when to apply more or less pressure. He took his time. He knew he had me in the palm of his hands. He stood up to grab a condom from his pant pocket. It was my turn to please him. I stood up and got on my knees. I grabbed his dick, looked up at him and smiled. He had this look on his face like he was ready to attack, like he was hungry for me. I took my tongue and circled the head a few times then I deep throated him until I gagged. He let out a soft moan and said, "Damn." I took one hand and cupped his balls and the other on the base of his dick and fucked him with my mouth until he pushed me away. "Get on the bed," he ordered. Shhhiddddd you ain't gotta tell me twice. I laid on my back while he put the condom on. He crawled on top of me and started kissing all over my breasts. He took my legs and folded me up like a lawn chair. This is that position that makes bitches show up at your mama's house acting a fool. I braced myself for the deep penetration. I felt the head of his penis at my opening. He gently pushed himself inside me. He opened me up and I welcomed him in. I moaned loudly as he pushed deeper and deeper. I looked at him and his face was full of passion and pleasure. He put one of my legs down and leaned in and kissed me. He then buried his head in my neck and stroked me perfectly for a cool minute until I felt my body heat up and release the deepest, strongest orgasm I ever felt. Once he saw that I came he switched up the position. He got on his knees and put one of my legs between his and the other on his shoulder and I was slightly turned on my side. He sped things up. He smacked my ass, then he reached down and put his hand around my neck and gently choked me. He choked me and stroked me a little more aggressive. Smack. His big hands smacked my ass again and I was in heaven. I wonder if he likes his eggs scrambled with cheese or over easy with a side of bacon. I could feel him getting ready to explode so I started throwing it back at him. He started to breathe heavily. A few more strokes and he started to come. I watched his sexy ass until he collapsed on the bed. We both laid there catching our breath. We looked at each other and smiled and I leaned over to kiss him and laid on his chest. After we caught our breath we started pillow talking. Laughing and talking about what just had happened. I looked up at him and he asked, "You want to hop in the shower with me?" "Of course." In the shower we flirted and explored each other's bodies. We got out and dried each other and that started round two and round two was just as good as round one. We got in the bed still talking, laughing and enjoying each other's company. We finally fell asleep holding each other.

CHAPTER 11

I woke up in a slight panic forgetting where I was. I looked over and saw Blu sleeping peacefully. The sun peeping through the blinds making his chocolate skin look edible. I thought about last night and how amazing it was. I smiled to myself. I stretched and scooted close to him and put my arm around him. I kissed his cheek. He smiled, eyes still closed and kissed me on the forehead and said in a sleepy voice, "Good morning." "Good morning." He got up and checked his phone. "Aw shit I gotta be at work at 12." He got up to go pee and I looked at my phone. It was 11:10 AM. I got up and put my dress on. I sat up on the bed and he came out of the bathroom half dressed. He ran and jumped on me in bed making me laugh. He hugged and kissed me. "You keep messing around and you won't make it to work," I joked. He got up and finished getting dressed, "I would rather have a round three right, but overtime is calling." He reached into one of the boxes on the floor and handed me a pair of Nike flops to put on. "Thank you cause I didn't want to do the walk of shame in my red hooker boots." He laughed. He finished getting dressed and grabbed his bag and we headed out the door together. We got to my car, he opened my door, and I hugged him, "I really enjoyed myself last night". He responded, "I could tell." He laughed. I was a little embarrassed. He read my mind again, "Don't be embarrassed you had me ready to tap out a few times." I smiled and as I got in the car he gave my ass a smack. I just sat there blushing and smiling showing all my damn teeth. He walked away, "I'll hit you up later." "Bye."

We pulled out his apartment. He was on the way to work and I was heading home. I grabbed my phone and saw I had no calls or texts from Lexi. I just shook my head. I dialed Jessica's number cause I was too excited to wait 'til I got home. As soon as she answered I just started screaming. I caught Jessica off guard, "Bre, what the hell? What's wrong?" I couldn't hold the water any longer, "Jesssss baabbbbaaae when I say Blu had my legs up in the air, I could have started C walking on the ceiling!" Jessica immediately changed her tone and got excited, "Girrlllll shut the front door!" "Yassssss sis!" I started singing, "I bet the neighbors know my name the way you screaming scratching yelling." "OMG shut up!" She was cracking up. "Wait how this happen, wasn't you with Lexi?" My excitement quickly went away, "She had me dressed and waiting in the car and she never answered the phone!" I said as I turned down my street. "What you mean? She stood you up? What happened?" I told Jessica what happened and the conversation I had with Lexi over the phone and how I ran into Blu. "Wow that's messed up." I was getting mad all over again, "I woke up to no text or calls from her, it was like she didn't even care." "Wait you in the car? You stayed the night with Blu?" I pulled into my garage. "Yep," I giggled. I grabbed my purse and got out of the car. "Ok now give me all the details from your night with Blu. Ayee my bestie got some cutty last night." I was laughing and having flashes of last night. I walked through my garage door and into my kitchen. Something was off. I looked around and I gasped. "Oh my God!" Jessica shaken by my voice said, "What is it?" I was frozen in place. I looked around trying to make sure I was seeing correctly, "Someone has broken into my house." Shit had been thrown around, drawers opened and emptied in my kitchen. Jessica yelled, "What?" As if she didn't hear me correctly the first time. I took a couple steps forward to get a better look. My furniture had been thrown everywhere and there were holes in the wall. I just stood there frozen, unable to move, unable to think, or speak. Jessica said calmly, "Bre get out the house, they could still be in there." I snapped out of it and I ran back through the garage door. I hit the button to open the garage door and got in my car, reversed out the driveway almost hitting my mailbox. I put it in drive and sped off damn near on two wheels. Jessica said in a concerned voice, "Bre, are you ok?" "I, I don't know. I can't believe this!" My heart was pounding and I was going 60 on a 40 mph street. I was breathing heavily and I just kept driving. "Bre, pull over somewhere!" I continued to drive, panicking and scared. Jesssica yelled, "Bre!" I finally responded, "Ok... ok" I pulled over into a 7-Eleven and parked. I caught my breath and gathered myself together. "Jessica, I need to call the police. I'll call you back. Jessica was panicking also, "Ok Bre just remain calm everything is going to be ok." "Ok." I hung up. Why me? This didn't seem real, I can't believe I was calling 911 to report a robbery that had taken place at MY house. "911 what's your emergency?" "My name is Bre and I think I have been robbed." My voice was shaky. "Ma'am are you still in the house?" "No, I walked in, saw that someone had been there and I got back in my car and left." I told the operator where I was and gave my address. "Ok, officer's are in that area and I will send them there now. Please stay where you are until the police arrive. Was there anyone else you know that was in the house?" "No, I live alone." The operator asked for more details of what happened and what I saw when I walked into my house. "Ok, police have arrived and are currently inspecting the scene." I began to relax a little. I lived in a quiet, safe neighborhood. How could this have happened? I'm not a flashy person on social media or in real life, so why would I be targeted? "Ma'am it is safe for you to head back to your home." "Ok, thank you." I hung up, took a deep breath, and began heading back to my house. My mind was racing. You hear about things like this happening to people but never would you think it would happen to you. What if who did this had been watching me and knew I wasn't going to be home last night? I felt so scared and alone. I wasn't sure I had even wanted to go back home. I tried not to let my thoughts get the best of me.

I pulled into my driveway and two police officers were talking in the front yard. I got out of the car and walked slowly to them making sure to make my hands visible. Although I called 911 and I was the owner of the house, I wasn't stupid to think I wouldn't be viewed as a criminal or suspect due to the color of my skin because we all know that Breonna Taylor died in her own home for no reason by the hands of the police. So I was always cautious when around OKCPD. The taller officer stated, "Are you Bre, the owner of this home." "Yes I called 911." The taller officer who I assume was the one in charge asked for my ID. On the ride over I got my ID out of my purse and had it in my hand ready. I handed my ID to the tall officer and he gave it to the shorter one and he went to his car probably to look up my information. The tall officer introduced himself as Officer Brady and said his partner's name was Officer Thompson. Officer Brady had me explain what happened so he could take my statement. He also informed me that no one was inside when they arrived. As we were talking I heard a car pull up in front of my house. I turned around to see who it was and it was Jessica. My best friend had come to be there for me and for support. I turned to the officer and let him know she was my friend and that I had been on the phone with her when I had walked in. Jessica approached me quickly, but cautiously, and hugged me, "Are you ok?" "I'm a little shaken up." Officer Thompson came back with my ID and asked me a couple more questions and then we went inside to do a walk through with me. Once inside Officer Brady asked, "Look around and see if you notice anything stolen. Do you have a safe?" "No," was the only word I managed to say while looking at the place I called home. It was a disaster. You would have thought there had been a tornado in there. As I looked around I didn't notice anything big taken. I still had my TV's and my laptop. I didn't really own any expensive jewelry and I just had a few big name brand clothing and shoes. Every drawer had been opened and all my clothes and shoes had been thrown around, but looked like nothing was taken. My mattress had been flipped and ripped open and pillows too. The tears I had been holding back started to fall. I looked at Officer Brady and asked how they got in. The shorter one spoke for the first time, "They somehow picked the lock on the back door and disarmed the alarm system. Whoever did it was some skilled professionals. This is something we don't see often. Do you have a camera security system?" "No. I had been meaning to do that a while ago but never got to it." I had lived here for three years and never took the time to update my security system. Once again, I didn't think this would happen to me. I looked at the back door and it was slightly ajar but looked like it hadn't been touched. Jessica came over and hugged me, "It's going to be ok, we can replace materialistic stuff, I'm just glad you wasn't here when it happened." I continued to look around. In the kitchen the cabinets and drawers had been opened, pots, pans, and dishes had been thrown everywhere, and most were broken. In the living room my furniture was flipped over and couch cushions were ripped up and the other rooms in my house looked the same way. I said out loud, "This doesn't make sense, doesn't look like anything was taken and why would some skilled robbers target me?" Officer Brady spoke, "Looks like they were looking for something, any idea of what?" "No, other than my TV's, laptop, and a few electronics I don't have anything of big value and like I said I don't have a safe and no one really knows where I live. And I don't have any enemies," I was confused. I felt disrespected, vulnerable, and exposed. Officer Thompson asked again if I was sure I didn't have any enemies. I thought about Drew, but he wouldn't have a reason to do this, what would have been the point in trashing my place, I hadn't seen or heard from him in weeks. He had blocked me from all social media so it's not like he knows what's going on in my life. So I told him no. "Since nothing was stolen and we have no possible suspects, it's going to be challenging to find out who did this, but we will do what we can. A police officer will be in the area tonight for your comfort." I thanked the officers and they left. I sat on the floor and cried. Jessica sat next to me.

CHAPTER 12

After I pulled myself together, I got up off the floor. Me and Jessica started cleaning. "We're gonna get through this together." I looked at my friend, "I really appreciate you coming to see about me and being here." "Now you know I will always be here for you." "Thanks," I smiled. I was thankful for our friendship. Most of my family lived in my home town of Okmulgee, OK and some lived in the Tulsa area, so having Jessica here was a big relief. I checked my phone and there were no missed calls or texts. I decided to call Lexi, her coming to help clean would be a start with me forgiving her for how she acted and part of me just wanted to be surrounded by my friends. I called, it rang a few times and went to voicemail. I smacked my lips as I set the phone down. Jessica was looking at me, "She probably did it." "What?" I stopped what I was doing and looked at Jessica. She continued, "Lexi either did this or had something to do with it." "Jess, I know you don't like her but damn..." Jessica cut me off, "Hear me out, she got you out the house and didn't show up so that's plenty of time to break in." "Ok, but nothing was stolen so what would be the point in that?" "I don't know, I just feel like she has something to do with it." I didn't have the energy to argue so I let it go.

Then I remembered Blu. I had such a beautiful night with him. The events of the day almost made me forget. A smile came across my face thinking about us on the dance floor and at his apartment. Jessica interrupted my thoughts, "You thinking about Blu? I know that's what you're smiling about. You never finished your story about what happened." I smiled a huge smile thinking about last night. I told her everything from getting freaky on the dance floor to us ending up at his apartment. "Aww shit my sis was doing the mostest last night." I laughed. Jessica added, "I can't believe Drew hasn't tried to come crawling back. Have you heard from him?" "No and I'm glad I haven't. Sometimes I do find myself wondering what he is doing or how he is doing but I just fight the urge to reach out to him." We cleaned up a little more, then Jessica took me to Wal-Mart to get an air mattress until I can get a new mattress. On the way to the store I got a text from Blu.

Blu: Wyd. I been thinking about you all day.

Bre: On my way to the store. You wouldn't believe what happened to me when I got home this morning.

Blu: What?

Bre: Someone broke into my house and basically trashed it.

One minute after I sent that text, he was calling. I answered, "Hello." "Bre, are you ok? What happened?" "Yes, I'm fine." I explained what happened when I got home. "Wow, I'm sorry. Who could have done this?" "That's the problem, I have no clue. Maybe they had the wrong house, I don't know." I was starting to fieel myself tear up again. "You want me to come stay with you tonight?" "That's sweet of you, but my friend Jessica is going to stay with me and plus my place looks terrible." "I don't care about that, I just don't want you to be alone. If you want I can come Monday, let me at least come check on you." "Ok, that sounds good." It was nice to know he cared to make sure I was good. "I'm about to be off work so call me if you need me." "Ok thanks." "Alright talk to you later."

We got to the store and got an air mattress, food, and wine. Afterwards we headed to Jessica's place so she could get some clothes to stay the night. Anya was with Jessica's mom, she begged to come with us, but we both knew it wasn't something she needed to see and we didn't want her to be worried. While on our way back to my place, my phone rang. It was Lexi. I answered, "Hello." "Hey Bre, I'm sorry about last night I had a lot of drama." "That's not a good enough reason to stand me up and then flip the script on me. I really thought we were better than that." Jessica whispered, "Ask where she was last night." I shot her a look and ignored her request. "Bre, I'm not perfect like you, I make mistakes. I said I was sorry." "You out of all people should know I am not perfect nor do I act like I am. What's been going on with you lately?" It was quiet for a moment. She finally spoke, "I don't know what else you want me to say." It was the first time I thought to myself maybe she wasn't a good friend. "Look, I was calling because someone broke into my house and trashed it." "Oh my God! Are you ok?" She said concerned. "Yeah, but I really needed my friends there for me. Jessica is here and just like last night you wasn't." "Bre, I'm so sorry. I didn't know..." Click. I hung up just like she hung up on me last night. Jessica yelled, "See, bitch ain't got no manners!"

We got back to my place and as I pulled into my garage I had this uneasy feeling. I didn't want to go in. I didn't feel comfortable. Jessica noticed my change in behavior, "You good?" "I don't know if I will ever feel comfortable in my own home again." "You want to stay in a hotel tonight?" I thought about it, but decided to toughen up and stay. We went inside and I had hoped that it had looked normal like nothing had happened and I was just dreaming. But no, I was standing in my living room and didn't have a place to sit because my couch was ripped up. I started to feel angry but I felt helpless. I couldn't do anything but move on and hoped that I would find out who did this and why. We threw a frozen pizza in the oven and blew up the air mattress to get ready for bed. We ate and I said a prayer for protection and went to sleep.

CHAPTER 13

It was Monday and here I am at work as if I wasn't completely violated yesterday. Jessica helped me clean up a lot last night and throw away stuff that was going to have to be replaced. Then we passed out on wine on the air mattress. Jessica tried hard to get me to take the day off, but I didn't want to be there and be reminded of what happened nor did I want to be alone. Plus I only had two clients today and I would feel bad rescheduling them. I managed to find some clothes to put on this morning and decided to make the best of the day. I called the officer to see if there were any leads or if he thought maybe it was a possibility that they had the wrong house. He ended up not being much help at all. My first client of the day was my sweet Mr. Johnson for his usual Monday appointment. We had a good session today, "Ok, Mr. Johnson, our time is up for the day, same time next Monday?" "Sounds good to me." I rescheduled him and prepared for my next client. I checked my phone and had two missed calls, one from Blu and one from Lexi. Blu had called me last night when he got home and this morning to check on me. He was worried about me and probably checking in on me again. Lexi had called and texted a few times, apologizing and asking if I was ok. I didn't respond at first but I eventually texted her back and told her I was ok. I started my session with my last client. She was a young woman who had been adopted and was dealing with abandonment issues. She had a breakthrough today during our session and was experiencing some clarity, feeling a little bit better about some of her circumstances and was having a better outlook on life. That in return made me glad I decided to come to work. It is very rewarding to see my clients make progress. I really loved helping people and I loved what I do.

After I was done with my last client, I sat in my office answering a couple emails and returning some calls. I was trying to decide if I should call my mom and update her. I didn't want to worry and get her upset but I thought just in case something else happened I should let her know. After I spoke with her I had to talk her out of coming to OKC to 'take care of her baby'. Then I called my dad and told him and before we got off the phone he was already searching for a good surveillance security system. I got off the phone with him and laid my head on the desk. I was mentally drained and tired because I didn't sleep too well last night.

On my way home I called Blu to see if we were still on for tonight. He suggested he could stop and get some takeout on the way over and I happily agreed. My kitchen was not in any condition to be cooking anything. He asked, "What you want to eat?" "You like Mexican food or maybe pizza?" "Mexican sounds good. You like Ted's?" "Yep." "Ok, text me your order and I will pick it up." I texted him my order and address and he said he will be at my place around six. When I got home I did my best moving stuff around to make it look less like a crime scene. Looking at the place I was still in disbelief. I didn't want to be here, but knowing Blu was coming made me feel better. The one furniture that wasn't ruined was my dining table which I was grateful for because we had somewhere to sit and eat. I got in the shower and put on some smell goods and lit some candles. I started to feel excited to see him again. I couldn't wait for him to get here so I could feel safe. I put something cute but comfortable on and I poured myself a glass of wine and played some music. I put the Summer Walker music station on.

Late at night, Eleven, we're cruisin'
Lately I been watchin' your movements
If I'm the only one that you're choosin'
Am I your favorite drug you've been usin'
                    (Eleven by Khalid)

I heard my doorbell ring. I walked to the door, I turned around to glance at the mess I called home and shook my head. I felt my eyes water up and a lump form in my throat. This was his first time at my place and this is what it looks like. Get it together, no time for a breakdown now. I glanced through the peephole and opened the door. Blu was standing there looking sexy as ever. He was holding two big bags of food. I took one of the bags. I kissed him and let him in, "Sorry about this mess..." He cut me off, "You bet not apologize for this and you saw what my place looked like." He made me laugh. I guided him to the table where he sat the food down and then gave me the best hug, a hug I didn't know I needed. I gave him a tour of the mess and told him how the officers said that the intruders were skilled because they were able to cut off my alarm. He was amazed at all the damage, "Wow, this is like a scene from a movie. I'm really sorry this happened to you. Can I help replace some of your things?" "Oh no, I appreciate it really, but I couldn't ask you to do that. I'm ok. I think I got everything." "At least let me buy you some new dishes." "If that is what you want to do, it would be greatly appreciated."

We sat down at the table and made our plates and ate. I poured him a glass of wine and poured myself a second glass. While cleaning up last night I found some old Uno cards so we played a few hands. We both did a lot of trash talking because he kept making up rules for the game. I was enjoying myself, he had took my mind off of everything. I took the last sip of my wine and got up from the table, "I gotta go to the ladies room." I got up and kissed him as I walked by him and he smacked my ass. I giggled and had slight chills go through my body.

That night still had my head spinning. I went to the bathroom that was in my bedroom. When I walked in there I looked to see if I could tell how tipsy I was. *You straight. You looking good.* I turned around to see how my ass was looking. *Yeah I need to get in the gym.* After a small heart to heart with myself. I used the bathroom. *Damn I'm pissing loud. I wonder if he can hear me. I probably shouldn't have had that last glass of wine.* I stood up from the toilet and lost my balance a little. I laughed at myself. When I was done I washed my hands and looked in the mirror, I was definitely buzzed from the wine. I guess I was a little stressed about everything and had a little too much to drink. I turned around and did a quick twerk in the mirror. I was about to go for a repeat of Saturday night. When I came out the bathroom he was standing in my room. I smiled and walked over to him seductively. He put his hands around my waist and squeezed me. He picked me up and spun me around. I was smiling from ear to ear. He put me down and he kissed me. He pulled back and looked me in the eyes and said, "I'm sorry." A little confused, I said, "For what?" He didn't respond, but I heard another voice laugh and say, "For this." Before I could turn around to see who said it. I felt a sharp pain in my head then everything went dark.

CHAPTER 14

I opened my eyes. My head was throbbing. Someone hit me on the head and knocked me out. Wait. Am I dreaming? I heard two people talking. I looked around. I was in my room on the floor next to my air mattress. This was real. I tried to scream for help but my mouth wouldn't move. It was taped. I tried to get up and run but my hands and feet were tied. What the fuck is going on? This has to be some type of joke or maybe some sex shit Blu was into. Either way this shit wasn't funny. I heard Blu say, "It's not her." Then I heard footsteps heading towards my room. It sounded like at least two other people was here. Who the hell else was here? Blu walked in my room first. Then another man walked in. My heart dropped into my stomach. I stopped breathing. I must've was seeing things but this couldn't be right. Right behind Blu walking into my room was my client, Mr. Johnson. The sweet old flirty man with the pinchable cheeks, was here, in MY house. I stared in disbelief, nothing was sweet about the look he had in his eyes. He looked as if he was a completely different person from when he would sit across from me in our sessions. There were two other men with him. My brain couldn't make sense of what I was seeing. Confusion wasn't the word. I looked at Blu for some type of explanation or some type of clue as to what was going on but I got nothing, just a blank stare. I stared at Blu and pleaded with my eyes for him to help me or at least explain what the hell was going on. Mr. Johnson ordered the other guys he was with to sit me up. They went into the kitchen and brought back a chair and sat it down and then they picked me up and sat me in the chair. I had never been this scared in my life, I had no clue what they were about to do to me. They sat me up straight in the chair and Mr. Johnson got close to my face. I noticed he had a gun in his pants. He said, "I'm going to take this tape off and ask you some questions. If you scream I will kill you. If you don't answer my questions or if you lie, I will kill you. Do you understand?" His voice was way different, it was monotone and low and creepy like a psychopath. He had been putting on a show at our therapy sessions as if he was an innocent older man with a comforting voice. But why? I nodded my head, huge tears falling down my face. He stepped back and one of the men he was with walked over and pulled the tape off my mouth. I still didn't understand what was happening. How did Blu and Mr. Johnson know each other? Was this whole thing a set up? Mr. Johnson stared at me for a moment and I sat still, unable to move because I was too scared. Finally he spoke, "I'm going to get right to the point. I run a business and I work very hard for the money that I make and one thing I hate is a thief." Thief? He continued, "I can respect a hustler making a way for him and his family but a THIEF really pisses me off. A thief takes the easy way out and takes what someone has worked hard for." I have no clue what he is talking about or why he is even saying this to me, but I remain quiet out of fear of him shooting me. He said, "You and your boyfriend stole from me and I am going to give you a chance to give me my product and money back because you seem like a nice woman, who maybe was dragged into this lifestyle out of some type of street, Bonnie and Clyde love story or some bullshit like that. I also have to admit when I started coming to you as a client, I did it to learn your whereabouts and to study my enemy, but surprisingly you actually helped me during some of the therapy sessions that I had with you." He laughed at himself. I looked over at Blu and he wouldn't even look me in the eye. I turned my attention back to Mr. Johnson who continued talking in a voice I wouldn't have believed was his a week ago unless I saw it with my own eyes, "So for that, instead of shooting first and asking questions later, I'm going to be nice." He stepped closer to me and bent down so that we were face to face. I was sweating and shaking uncontrollably. "Where is my money and products?" I was scared shitless, I couldn't even get my words together. I started stuttering, trying to talk. SMACK. He slapped me damn near out the chair. I felt my cheek swell up and he grabbed me by my chin and yanked my face back facing him and said through clenched teeth, "You better get your story together because I am missing $350,000 in cash and $450,000 in product and I need my shit yesterday." I started sobbing and Blu still just stood there letting this man do this to me. I took a deep breath and talked through the pain and tears, "Mr. Johnson.." He cut me off, "My name is James." "James, I am not a thief and I would never steal from anyone and I don't have a boyfriend, I think you have the wrong person." He sighed as if he was disappointed in my answer, he stood up straight and he pulled out his phone. He started going through his phone as if he was looking for something. I looked at Blu and started begging, "Blu, please tell him I didn't do anything, this has to be a mistake." Blu looked as if he wanted to say something but didn't. He just took a deep breath and stared at me. I closed my eyes tight and said a quick prayer. I was about to die for no reason and the guy I was starting to fall for, lied and set this up. James found whatever he was looking for on his phone. He put the phone in my face to show me what was on it. It was a video. He pressed play. The video was a surveillance camera that looked to be located on a building of a gas station at a truck stop, it was night time and it was kind of faraway, but I could still make out what I was seeing, the area was lit from the lights at the store. As the video played I saw several 18 wheeler trucks lined up and I saw Blu get out one of them and walk towards the gas station. Moments later a black SUV pulled up on the driver's side of the truck. The way the truck was parked, the passenger side faced the store, so when Blu came out the store he would not see the SUV. James fast-forwarded the video and

59

stopped when he saw Blu walking back to the truck. Blu walked back to the driver's side with snacks in hand to get back in his truck not realizing the SUV was parked, waiting for him. I couldn't see what was happening due to the truck blocking the view from the camera but it was obvious something was going on. About a minute later Blu comes back in the camera's view at the rear of the truck and Drew was right behind him with a gun pointed in his direction dressed in all black with a black bandana around his mouth. At first I didn't recognize him cause he usually kept his hair cut low but looked like he was in the beginning stages of growing dreads. The person I have been trying to get away from has come back into my life and brought more drama with him. Drew and Blu started conversing back and forth, which was obvious through body language. Drew must have told Blu to open the trailer because Blu started to open it. It looked like he and Drew started arguing again and Drew put the gun close to his head, which caused Blu to put his hands up as if he was saying he surrendered. Seconds later a van pulled up and backed up to where its rear was facing the rear of the truck. Three men dressed in all black got out the van and started walking towards Drew. Out of nowhere a woman with a black ski mask came from around the truck where the SUV was parked and walked over to Drew and kissed him. She was dressed in all black too. She was tall and had chocolate skin like me. You would have thought she was my sister. It was Jessica. My best friend. I recognized her walk and body language anywhere, it was no doubt her. My best friend. MY. BEST. FRIEND. My day one had just walked up and kissed my ex and was committing a robbery with him. What in the entire fuck! In the video Jessica motioned for the men who got out the van to hurry and take whatever it was that was in his trailer. He stopped the video and stared at me. I felt like I was going to faint. I started to feel nauseous and dizzy. I couldn't do anything but cry, I had snot falling from my nose and I could barely see from the tears that poured out my eyes. "It's not me," I said in between tears, "It's not me, please believe me! I had nothing to do with that! Don't kill me!" Blu finally spoke, "Boss, it's not her, different body type." I looked at this motha fucka crazy, like you seriously want to say something NOW after he had slapped the shit out of me. I looked at Blu and screamed, "Fuck you!" I was coughing and gagging from crying so hard. James stood with his arms crossed and rubbing his chin as if he was thinking. Blu could see the hurt in my eyes and he walked into the bathroom and came out with some tissue to wipe my face. He took the tissue and reached towards my face and I opened my mouth and bit down on his hand as hard as I could. He yelled, put his fist up and was about to hit me but stopped himself. I let go of his hand and gave him a look I wished could have killed him. James must was entertained because he had a good laugh, "Come on Blu, don't tell me you fell for this girl or are you getting soft? What would your wife think?" Shocked, I said, "You're married?" I couldn't take this anymore, it was all so overwhelming. Blu's face cringed slightly and you could tell he was upset that James had said that. I felt nothing but rage. My best friend had betrayed me, Blu had lied and set me up, and my ex is the reason for all this shit. I made a promise to myself that If I got out of this alive I was going to come for all of them and I wasn't going to hold back even if that meant I would be in jail. These bitches, especially Jessica, was going to pay for this. Blu went into the bathroom and came back with his hand bandaged up. How did he know where my bandages were? Has he been in my house before? James was back serious, "So Bre, after taking a closer look at the video, I see that Blu is right, it's not you, but your reaction to the woman in the video tells me you know her. Who is she?" I hesitated. Although Jessica deserved this ass whooping I was going to give her, I was afraid to tell him her name because I wasn't sure what he was going to do to her and I couldn't live with myself if something happened to Anya. "I don't know." I lied.

James charged at me. Blu yelled, "Wait!" But it was too late. James punched me in the stomach and it knocked all the wind out of me. I was gasping for air and bent over in pain. "It's her friend, I saw her leave here this morning." Blu spoke up. I shot him an evil look. No telling how long he had been following me. "Well why didn't you say that." James looked irritated. "I just now put it together," Blu replied. I started panicking, I didn't want anybody to die. James got close to me again and looked at me with an emotionless, blank, face. I stiffened up to prepare for the next blow but he just said, "I need you to find Drew and introduce me to your friend."

and I've seen him beat a teenage boy into a coma for being "disrespectful". I wasn't worried for myself though. I felt there wasn't a way I could mess this up. I was working a legit job and was just carrying extra cargo that I didn't even have to touch. It was too easy. Soon my son came and my wife was happy with her new life. The money gave us a way of life that one could only dream of. Jada was able to be a stay at home mom and we took a lot of family vacations and owned nice things. Things were going good and everything was perfect. Where there is sunshine and flowers, there is rain and storms.

Jada started to change. When I first met Jada, she was a materialistic person who loved to show off or portray a certain lifestyle on social media. Whether it was makeup, clothes, or hairstyles, she would always post her life and what she had on the internet, it was sometimes annoying, but tolerable. After I started working for James and bringing in more money it got worse. It was like her love and affection for me turned into her love for red bottoms, Birkins, and jewelry. Jada was a smoker which is something I had accepted about her when we first started dating, but weed started to turn into pills and from pills to coke. At home she never had to lift a finger to cook, clean, or even raise our son. She breast fed our son for about a month and then hired a nanny. Our marriage had turned into me being a bank and her living her best life and our son being raised by the nanny. I was there to raise him as much as I could despite my crazy work schedule. When I wasn't working I had him. I made sure he went to doctor's appointments, made sure he was cleaned and fed, and I took him out to the park and we did lots of other activities. Jada was lazy and would rather have the nanny do everything. As quick as I made the money she was spending it. She spent it on her family, friends, and materialistic things that helped her to keep up with the internet lifestyle she had made for herself. She was always either out partying or hosting a party at our home. When I confronted her she

64

CHAPTER 15

Blu

I have been a truck driver transporting goods for companies for almost nine years. One day about three years ago, I met James at a truck stop and he approached me offering me a job to make some extra money. He said all I had to do is keep working like I normally do except that I would be transporting something extra to the surrounding states on my normal truck routes. I wish I would have turned him down back then, but I was deep in debt from using school loans, medical bills, and credit cards and a few bad choices I had made earlier in life and my wife, Jada, was expecting our first child. So I didn't think twice about it. I figured I could do it for a while until I can get on my feet and buy a house for my family. I started moving weight for James and the money was good and I barely had to do anything. I would meet his people at a truck stop, they would load up the product and I would meet at a different truck stop in another state and his people would be there waiting to unload it. After working with him for a few months I never had any issues and James began to trust and respect me. The loads got bigger and it became more than just drugs. I would transport money, guns, and equipment along with weed, coke, and pills. The money increased with the bigger shipments. I was bringing in 5K a week. In a year I was able to get out of debt and buy a house. I knew dealing with anything drug related, there was a dark side. I told myself it wasn't my business and I would turn a blind eye to it. The longer I worked with James the more I saw how ruthless he was. I saw him snap a man's neck over fifty dollars would blame me for my long hours on the road and me not giving her enough attention and feeling alone. What she didn't realize was she was slowly putting us back in debt. I tried to get her to calm down on the spending but all she would say is, "Ask your boss for more money. You been putting in work for him for years, he needs to give you a raise." She started to feel entitled to the lifestyle and she was dependent and couldn't take care of herself and had no motivation to do anything. One day I had come home to a party at my house while my son was there. We got into a big argument in front of everybody. She was drunk and high and our son was in the other room unattended. I made everyone leave. But the moment I knew our marriage was over is when I came home early one weekend, Jada and a guy that I knew was passed out half naked with pills and coke all over the table. Thankfully my son was with his grandma, but about the time she and the guy woke up from their high, I had her bags packed sitting outside. And what she didn't know is that I had took pictures of them and the drugs while they were passed out in case I needed proof she was an unfit mother. I wasn't going to allow her to take my son from me. I had enough friends who dealt with spiteful, bitter ex-wives and baby mamas to know I needed to document and have proof of situations like this cause at the end of the day I wasn't going to be paying child support for a child that I supported. We have been separated for the last two months. I had been trying to get her to sign the papers for our divorce, but she would refuse to. She had insisted we work it out, but I had already fell out of love with her and I was done trying. She stayed at her mom's house until she figured out what she was going to do because she wasn't allowed back at my house. My son mostly stayed at my mom's house and even though she was allowed to come see him whenever she wanted, she didn't come much unless she needed some money. She would use him to get money out of me. I let it slide and gave her money while I secretly worked with a lawyer to get full custody and supervised visits. I had given her the world and she didn't do nothing but use me and disrespect me. I began to wonder if she had ever loved me from the beginning.

About a month ago I was working and it was like any other day. I had just picked up a load and was heading to Texas. It was late at night and I had to pee and was hungry. I usually would have pushed through to get to my destination, but I had had an extra cup of coffee before my shift started due to being up half the night arguing with Jada. So I decided to pull over at the next stop. My first and only mistake. It was summer time, people were partying more and due to the high demand of drugs, my load was a little bigger than usual. I pulled in, parked, and headed to the store. When I came out Drew was waiting for me on the side of the truck with a gun. My gun was in the truck. I was pissed he caught me slippin. I had recognized Drew instantly. I would hear James and his workers talking about him and how he was being reckless in the streets and how he was a hot head that cared too much about chasing pussy than money. He was sloppy with his work and wasn't respected. One day they were talking about him and one of James's guys was showing the other guys Drew's Instagram pictures. They were laughing at him. I happened to be nearby and the guy wanted me to join in on the laugh so he showed me the pictures. There were pictures of him showing off money and guns and pictures of him smoking and with strippers. Just a lot of immature shit that helps make the police's job easier. Real street men don't have to do it for the gram. I remembered in the pictures he had a small tattoo on the side of his face and I remember thinking I don't understand why people got face tattoos, especially people in the streets, where they can be easily identified. Here he was pointing a gun at me but I led him to think that I didn't know who he was. He made me open my trailer. I didn't get a good look at her, but it was obviously his girlfriend by the way they were kissing that had helped him. All I could think was how

James had snapped that guy's neck for 50 damn dollars. I was scared for the first time since starting this. More so scared for my son because I couldn't leave him to be raised by his mother, without me, she could barely take care of herself. But I had Drew's name and I was going to find out who his girlfriend was and make them both pay because I wasn't ready to die, at least not without a fight.

That phone call to James was one of the scariest things I ever had to do in my life. I had to tell him I allowed someone to rob him of almost a million dollars worth of stuff. I called and explained to him what happened and he was silent for what seemed like forever. "Boss, it was Drew and his girlfriend, give me a chance to find them and get your stuff back." He just hung up. A cold chill went through my body, I knew this wasn't going to be good, but luckily I knew he was in Mexico getting more product and making some connections and I knew he wouldn't be back for a few days. I used this opportunity to find out everything I know about Drew and his girlfriend. After some investigation on social media and asking some people on the streets, I found out his girlfriend's name was Bre. It was hard to find where Drew was located because people were not willing to tell that much but I found Bre easily. She was a well-known therapist and with a quick google search I found where she had her practice. One day I camped outside her building to get a good look at her. I saw her leaving her office and walking to her car. I could tell it was her from the pictures from Facebook. I took note of her car and license plate. I couldn't deny how beautiful she was. She seemed to have a great career so I couldn't understand why she would help somebody like Drew rob somebody else. I was confused on why she would even be with a man like him. It didn't matter though, I was ready to hand her and Drew's life over to James. It was either them or me and my son. And I also wanted revenge. Drew had put a gun to my head and they had robbed me and put my life in danger. That shit was upsetting me and my homeboys, and they needed to pay for that.

A couple days had gone by and I could not find Drew anywhere. It was almost like he disappeared or maybe he was laying low after the robbery. As for Bre, she continued on with her life like it was nothing, like she didn't care that she just placed a target on my head. After following her, she mostly went to work and came home. There was no sign of her meeting up with Drew or being involved in his business on the streets. I was at home one day when I heard a knock on the door. It had been three days since I talked to James on the phone. I looked through the peephole and saw that it was one of James' security, Kash. James had two right hand men that did most of his dirty work and was his muscle, Kash and Ben. They didn't talk much, they just did as they were told. Word on the street was they were his sons but that was never confirmed. I took in a deep breath and opened the door. Kash, who was tall and muscular like a football player told me to get in the car. I got in the car and Ben was driving. Ben was shorter and slimmer but was quick and strong. He was an amazing boxer and if he would have played his cards right he could have gone pro, but the streets had a tight grip on him. During the drive I thought about my life, my son, and my mistakes. I thought I would have had more time to find Drew, but looks like James cut his trip short and came to take care of me. We drove to a shopping center and went inside a vacant building on the eastside of town. Inside there was a table and two chairs. James sat in one of them. Then Kash motioned for me to have a seat. I sat and waited for him to speak. He stared at me with a look of disappointment. "I like you Blu." He paused, but I kept quiet, I knew better than to interrupt him. He continued, "You never gave me any problems and you never asked me any questions or asked me for anything. You helped make me a lot of money and have made my transactions easier, but I'm disappointed you let your guard down and allowed this to happen." This was it, I was about to die in this building and my son would grow up without a father and be raised by his selfish dependent mother. James didn't say anything and continued to stare at me. If I could only go back to that day, but I said yes to the money, and now I only hoped for a quick death and pray that my mother would take care of my son. He asked, "So what information have you gathered?" I was surprised, he never gave second chances, and he hardly gave people time to explain. "I was able to find his girlfriend Bre and where she lives and works but I cannot find where Drew is hiding." He replied, "Drew has been fucking things up for me lately and word on the street is he is trying to come for my spot. So today Blu, I need you alive. You are going to get Bre to tell you where he is." I was hoping I could just give him names and locations and hand it over to him. I didn't want to be involved. I wasn't cut out for this life and I didn't want any blood on my hands, but it was my fuck up so I guess I had to put in the work to make it right. The last thing I was going to do is tell him no or question him after he spared my life. James stood up from the table, "In the meantime I will visit Bre at her job and learn a little bit more about her since she wants to play Bonnie and Clyde." James knew he had taken a loss in what was stolen from him, but I see he was willing to let the little fish go so he could catch the big fish. I knew he wanted his drugs back, but I also know he wanted to bring an end to Drew and his crew. Before he walked off he pulled a picture out of his pocket and sat it on the table in front of me. It was a picture of my son playing outside at his daycare. I knew what that meant. That meant me and my son was being watched and I couldn't run. I had to do this for him or else he would kill both of us. I was escorted back to the car and dropped off back at home. Once I shut my door and his security had driven off, I dropped to my knees and thanked God for giving me another chance and I went to go get my son.

A couple weeks went by and James had me back transporting drugs and money trying to make up for the loss. I had stopped following Bre and concentrated on making money to put away for me and my son in case of an emergency. James started seeing Bre as a client, while his people searched for Drew. I realized James wasn't having much luck when he called me on a Saturday night and told me he needed me to get close to Bre. That was the last thing I wanted to hear. "James, I..." "You don't have an option." He hung up. I sat on my bed to try to think of ways to get out of this. Flashes of that picture of my son kept coming to my mind. I had to get close to Bre and end this whole thing.

That next morning I was at her house watching trying to figure out how I was going to do this. I would have to find a way to get her to trust me. As I sat across the street I saw her and a shorter girl leave her house in separate cars. I saw Bre and got upset again. I remember that night at the truck stop they were all kissy and lovey dovey during the whole thing and I was disgusted. I followed Bre. She went to have breakfast at this café off Memorial. She went inside to eat and I had to think quickly. James had given me this tracking device to put on her car. I waited a while to give her a little time to order and eat. Then I got out of the car and went to hers. I bent down and taped the tracking device under her car. My heart was beating fast and I was nervous. I had never done any shit like this. I said a prayer to God asking if he got me out this situation I would get my life together. I stood up and took a step back to view the car to see if the tracker was visible and as I was looking Bre was walking towards me. Perfect timing, I had already had my lie together, I would say that I was looking for my mask. She approached me but kept her distance. I turned my charm on and got her smiling and was able to get her number. Seeing her up close I was able to get a good look at her and she was sexy and definitely the type of woman I would have approached if the circumstances were different. But she was a thief and probably the type that chased money and drugs like my soon to be ex-wife. On the inside I replayed that moment at the truck stop and got angry again. Her time will come.

We went on a date about a week later and I surprisingly had a great time. She was smart and funny and had a good head on her shoulders. From what she would say about Drew it seemed like they weren't together or communicating which couldn't have been true. But I had to be careful and not make it too obvious that I was trying to get information about him. While I was getting to know her I had to keep reminding myself that she was lying and that she wasn't a good person. It was a little frustrating and confusing because she seemed so genuine. This was no doubt the girl that had helped Drew but at the same time her personality didn't fit the girl I thought she was. Our date was Friday evening and that Saturday morning I got a call from James saying that we needed to step it up and couldn't waste any more time. That night I decided to use the tracker to my advantage. I started to feel uneasy about what I was doing, but I reminded myself this was for my son. I would do anything for him. James needed me to keep her out overnight so he could search her house. I told him I didn't want to bring her to my house. James owned a couple apartment complexes which he used some of the apartments for business transactions. He had an apartment that I could use. I went to get keys and check the place out and I took a few things there myself like clothes, tooth brush and towels. The only furniture was a bed and there were a few things in the kitchen and bathroom. I stood in the bathroom and looked at myself in the mirror. How did I get here? It was one thing to take her on a date but to sleep with her was crossing the line. I thought maybe I could get her over here and we can just talk. I had deceived this woman and tricked her. I started to feel guilty. After all it was my fault. I didn't have to stop at that truck stop AND I didn't have my gun on me, but I was already in too deep. I could tell she liked me and trusted me. I couldn't deny the chemistry my damn self. She was easy to talk to and be around. I just shook my head, took a deep breath and got those thoughts out of my head. I knew James wouldn't think twice on killing my son. I had to do this.

That night I switched to my old car. I didn't want her or anyone else to see me in my everyday car. We had talked on the phone and she told me she was going out but she didn't say where. I got dressed as if I was going out and checked the GPS tracker. It showed her heading to downtown OKC. I hopped in the car and wasn't about five minutes behind her. I had planned on "casually" bumping into her while she was out with her friends and somehow inviting her to stay with me. I just hoped that James and his crew found whatever they needed to find at her place. I wanted this shit to be over and wanted my life back to normal. I was able to catch up with her, she was parked in a parking lot, and I parked a couple rows back with a good view of her. I turned my engine off and sat and waited. I hoped she would go out and party and maybe have a few drinks and I could bump into her as she was leaving, but it seemed like something was wrong. She had sat in the car for almost 30 minutes. I started to panic. What if she changed her mind and went home. I had to think quickly and change the plan. I got out of the car and started walking towards where she was parked. She was about to pull out the parking spot and I knocked on the window. I had scared her and the look on her face was hilarious. After I stopped laughing I apologized for scaring her. She ended up telling me her friend had stood her up and she was pretty upset. It was easy to get her to still go out with me since she was already dressed and out. I suggested we still go have a few drinks and party. We got to the club and I had showed off a little bit by getting us in without any waiting or having to pay. I was good friends with the bouncer so he had no problems with letting us in and I knew he wouldn't ask any questions when he saw I wasn't with my wife. He just smiled and let us in. We had some drinks and we danced. The drinks helped some of my nerves to go away. For a minute I forgot about everything. I was having such a good time with her dancing that for a second I forgot about what was happening. It was like I was just out with my girl having a good time. She was looking good in her dress and red boots and the way she danced it was turning me on. Her body was beautiful, everything about her was beautiful. Maybe if I would have met her years ago, before she met Drew, we could have had something. She was everything that I wanted in a wife, complete opposite of Jada. Maybe Drew forced her to do it, that would have made more sense and maybe she really did break up with him because she was done with it. So many things were going through my mind. The DJ changed up the pace and played a slow song. I can tell she was feeling her drink by the way she was touching me. I knew she wanted me. I wanted her too. It had been almost four months since I had been with a woman and the way she looked at me, I could tell that was about to change tonight. I managed to talk her into following me to the apartment. *I have to do this for my son.* I kept repeating to myself as I drove. We got to the apartment and she believed the lie about the furniture. She trusted me. Her house was probably getting broken into at this very moment because of me, but she trusted me. In the bedroom it got heated quick. She was unbuckling my pants and I stopped her. I stared into her eyes. I liked her. *Just tell her the truth.* I should have just flat out asked where Drew was and the money and drugs, but there was a big chance she would get upset and leave or call the police or let Drew know we were looking for him. So I didn't, I let it happen and I would be lying if I said I didn't want it to happen. I just didn't want it to happen like this. I was attracted to her for sure. My body was calling for her and I couldn't stop myself after I saw her naked. It turned out to be the best sex I ever had. I was amazed by her skills and passion. Afterwards we laid in bed holding each other and it had been a while since I felt this type of connection with a woman. We had another round and we passed out naked under the sheets. That morning I pretended I had to go to work and we parted ways. I was anxious to talk to James to see if he found what he was looking for. I knew that Bre was going to be walking into her home any minute now and see what had happened. I got home and I sat there and waited impatiently for a call from either

James or Bre. I waited for her to call me to tell me what I already knew, that someone had broken in. It was the longest day of my life. Bre didn't call me as quickly as I thought she would, but then again she was probably torn up about what had happened and I still hadn't heard from James. Bre eventually called and told me what happened. She was really upset but she said her friend was with her and was going to be with her tonight and I offered to be there for her tomorrow. I did that not because James wanted me to be there but out of guilt. Hearing her sounding sad made me sad.

James called me later that night and said that they didn't find anything and word was Drew was out of town laying low and meeting with a team to start moving the weight he had stolen. I was disappointed. That meant something bad was about to happen to Bre. James said on the phone, "We are going to get to the bottom of this tomorrow night. You're going to go over there and let me in so I can confront her. I was able to get the surveillance video from the convenience store at the truck stop. I will show it to her in case she try to lie." "Wait..," click. He hung up. I didn't know there was a video of the incident. He wanted me to be there and let him in. That meant she would know I was connected to all of this. The truth would come out. I told myself at least this can all be over. I hope Bre will just give up Drew and James will just deal with him but that would be too easy. Maybe I could negotiate something. Fuck! This whole thing was insane. I didn't want to be there. I didn't want to see the look on her face when she saw it was me. I thought about running, but his men would be on me and my son before we could hit the highway. I had to face this. I had to face her. The woman that robbed me and that I now cared about.

I got up early that morning to camp out in front of her house. I don't know why I was there. I think I was looking for a reason to believe she wasn't as innocent as she acts and I also hoped that Drew would pop up and I just could take him to James and leave Bre out of it. Around 7:00 AM the garage door opened and I could see Bre and her friend get in their cars to leave. *Damn they kind of look alike.* Then all of a sudden I got a pain in my chest and stomach. I watched Bre's friend get into her car and pull out the driveway and I took another look at her as she drove off. I thought back to the night of the robbery, I tried to visualize the girl kissing Drew. Bre and her friend both were literally the same height and had the same chocolate skin. That night at the truck stop my adrenaline was pumping and I had a gun to my head. Was it possible that it wasn't Bre and her friend was the one that helped Drew! That kiss they shared was definitely a kiss from two people who have been together for a while. What if I was wrong? What if Bre was innocent this whole time? *Fuck!* I punched my steering wheel. Ok think...think. The video. I need to see that surveillance video to be sure or else an innocent person is going to be hurt and the person responsible will get away. I waited until after they left and I drove off to find James. I couldn't just call him because he always called me from a private number. He never wanted people to be able to get a hold of him, only the people real close to him were able to contact him. I went to a few spots where I thought he would be at and he wasn't there. Not even any of his crew were around. I went to the apartment that I was at the night before and he wasn't there and I checked another apartment complex and he wasn't there. I went home to think. I was home pacing the floor. I texted Bre to check on her, but no response, she probably was busy at work. I went to go pick up my son from daycare and take him to my mom's house. I got home and made myself a drink. I was stressed and I was all out of plans. I had to see the video. A part of me was happy to know that it might not be Bre and that she wasn't the woman I thought she was. I decided I would go over there tonight and see what happens. If anything I will look at the video to verify and tell James then. I just hope I won't be too late.

I'm on my way to Bre's house after I had picked us up some food. I hadn't heard from James. Maybe something came up or my prayers were answered and he found Drew. I just wanted this night to not go left and I hope James was willing to talk first. I got there and her place was completely wrecked. James and his crew did not hold back. You could tell she was embarrassed and sad but I was going to try my best to cheer her up. My guilt was eating me up. After looking around her place I thought how this could possibly be all for nothing. We sat at the table which was probably the only furniture she had left in good condition and we ate and played games but I couldn't completely relax knowing that James knew where she stayed. I knew he could pop up at any time. I toyed with the idea of telling her the truth, but I wasn't a hundred percent sure if it was her or her friend. While we were having drinks, James texted me and said him, Kash, and Ben were outside the front door. I put my phone down and looked at her, she was smiling completely clueless as to who I really was and what was happening. My stomach started to feel upset. I'm surprised she didn't notice the change in my behavior because I was having a hard time trying to act normal. She was a little tipsy though. She excused herself to the bathroom. As soon as she was out of site, I ran to the door and let him in and started talking quickly, "James I think I made a mistake. Do you have the video?" Him and his crew came inside. He completely ignored my question and asked, "Where is she?" "She is in the bathroom. Can I see the video please?" I begged. He held his hand up for me to stop talking, "I'm here now so let me handle it." I saw that he was getting frustrated. But I needed to see to make sure I wasn't tripping. It could be Bre or it could be her friend who betrayed her, I just wasn't sure. There wasn't time to talk, she was going to be coming out the bathroom any second now. James instructed me to wait for her in her room, for when she came out, and they would wait outside the room. Everything was happening so fast I couldn't think. I couldn't explain. I heard her washing her hands. *Shit.* James and his goons were outside the room and had guns and I felt helpless but I had to play this cool. I knew he wasn't going to kill her right away because he wanted to know where Drew was. She opened the bathroom door and saw me and smiled the sexist smile I had ever seen. The look in her eyes told me she was ready to take my clothes off. She walked towards me. I held her, picked her up and spun her around. I wasn't sure of what was going to happen but I wanted to see what was coming. All I could manage to say to her was, "I'm sorry." She looked confused and said, "For what?" "For this," Kash came in quick and knocked her out without thinking twice and Ben came in behind him to tape her mouth and tie her hands and feet. I was mad as fuck. That wasn't even necessary, she was a woman, and all they had to do was have a conversation with her. I could see that they wasn't here to do much talking. She was knocked out cold. While they tied her up I used this as an opportunity to try to talk to James. "James I really need to see that video." James reluctantly pulled out his phone, hit a few buttons, and handed it to me. We were all standing in the kitchen by now and Bre was in her room on the floor, tied up, still unconscious. They watched me watch the video. I fast forwarded until I saw the woman appear. I took a good look at her. The girl in the video was slimmer than Bre. It wasn't her. I was wrong. All this time she was a good woman. She was being honest and I had come into her life and messed it up for no reason. I remember when I first saw her, I had judged her and thought negative of her and she was innocent. She got tied up with the wrong guy, found the strength to leave him, and was trying to move on with her life. I looked at James, "It's not her." He was quiet, I couldn't tell what he was thinking. I knew I wasn't going to be given another chance. I just shook my head and said again, "It's not her."

We heard Bre waking up. James grabbed his phone from me and put it in his pocket. He motioned for me to go into the room. I walked in first and right behind me was James, then his boys. The look on her face when she saw James with me was terrifying. When she looked at me there was so much confusion and hurt in her eyes. It was hard for me to look her in the eyes. I had the wrong woman. If it wasn't for my mistake she would be in her bed sleeping peacefully. I had really fucked up. They sat her up in a chair from the kitchen and took the tape off her mouth. I stood by and watched the whole thing. Every once in a while she looked at me with anger and disappointment and I didn't blame her. James could be very intimidating and scary so when he asked her about the money and drugs, she was so scared she couldn't talk. James had slapped her and it took everything in me not to charge at him and I would have been shot dead by Ben or Kash in seconds. I felt like a coward, but I knew my son was being watched right at this moment. He would kill me and then make the call to kill him. I just looked at her and prayed that we would both make it out alive. Bre glanced at me again, still in shock at what I had done and at what was happening. James showed her the video and she broke down and pleaded with us that it wasn't her. I had spoken up and once again said it wasn't her and that the body type was different. Bre yelled at me and was crying hard. I was completely responsible for her pain, I was so caught up in what had happened and trying to protect me and my son that soon as I got a name for the girlfriend, I went with it. I didn't try to confirm it and I didn't consider that it could be someone else. I just wanted to give James the names so I could be free from the whole situation but I had the wrong person. Feeling like shit I went to grab tissue to wipe her face and she bit the shit out of me. She looked like she was ready to kill me. I didn't blame her so I brushed it off because I deserved worse. James realized I was right about it not being Bre, but Bre's face told it all, so he knew from her reaction that she knew who it was. She obviously had no clue that her friend was with her ex, but I can tell Bre didn't want to say who it was on the video. She had more balls than I did. When she didn't give the answer he wanted, James lunged at her so quick, punched her in the stomach before I could say I knew who it was. I was disgusted and lost any respect that I had for him. I spoke up then, because this had to stop. I told him that it was her friend and I had seen her here. Bre didn't know how ruthless he was like I did. The way I saw it she could either be beaten to death or give away a friend that obviously didn't give a damn about her. And I couldn't watch him put his hands on her anymore. Bre informed us that Drew had blocked her from all social media and blocked her number so she had no way of getting in contact with him and doesn't know where he is. James got Bre's cell phone and ordered her to call Jessica on the phone and put it on speaker. He wanted Bre to get her to say where Drew was and he also wanted Bre to try to get her to come over. Bre did her best to remain calm and act normal. She dialed her number and she answered after the first ring.

Bre: Hey girl, whatcha doing?

Jessica: Hey you ok, what's wrong?

Bre: Nothing, I was just in my feelings thinking about Drew, but I can't get in contact with him. You have his number?

There was a brief silence on Jessica's end.

Jessica: No. I thought you were with Blu tonight?

Bre: He left...

This time Bre hesitated. James pulled his gun out and held it to scare her.

Jessica: Hello? Is everything ok?

We all stood there waiting for her response. Bre looked at me and I whispered, "Please."

Bre: Yes. Can you come over?

Bre's voice was shaky, the pressure was on her.

Jessica: Bre, it's late. I got work in the morning and I got Anya. What's going on?

Bre: I just really need you. Can you take Anya to her dad's?

Jessica: Bre you're scaring me. Just tell me what's going on?

Bre: I just don't want to be alone tonight after the break in. Please.

Jessica: Ok I'll take Anya to her dad's house and I'll be over.

Bre: Ok thanks.

James smiled and put the gun down and said, "Looks like we are going to have a party."

CHAPTER 16

Jessica

I had an appointment to meet with the realtor to close on my dream home. So much had happened within the last month. I had come up on a lot of money and all because of my baby Drew. Me and Drew's relationship started a little over a year after him and Bre were together. At first we were just two friends that had a relationship with a mutual person we both cared about, then when things started to get rocky between him and Bre he would confide in me. He would complain that Bre was trying to change him and make him into someone he was not. I was secretly jealous of Bre's relationship with Drew. So when he would come to me with their problems, I welcomed it and didn't tell her. I was jealous because he was a good man who just wanted to take care of her but she was always nagging and complaining about stupid shit. She didn't deserve that attention, I did. I never had a man to do for me like Drew did for her. After me and Anya's dad didn't work, I had a hard time finding someone to help me and be there for me. I always had to work two jobs to make ends meet. I didn't finish college like Bre, it just wasn't for me. So I worked bullshit jobs trying to stay ahead. Bre changed after she graduated from college. She was always flaunting her degree around and once she started her practice, she didn't really have much time for our friendship anymore. We used to be so close growing up, but now she acts like she is too good for me and too good for Drew. When she met Lexi and started to let her hang with us I should have stopped fucking with her then. Lexi was childish and annoying but for some reason she cared about her on some mother daughter type bullshit and that would piss me off. I would see Drew check me out sometimes when we were all together. One night Bre was bitching again and he hit me up and wanted to come over. Drew was as sexy as they come. He was 6'3" with light caramel skin. He had a slim athletic build and he was the man in the streets. I had always wanted him. That day he approached Bre at Juneteenth on the east side, I was heartbroken. That night when I invited him over I knew what he wanted and I knew what I wanted. I was going to give him what he deserved. I wanted to show him I was the better woman and with me he wouldn't have to change. I could be his ride or die. As time went on we kept seeing each other on the low and I started to fall in love with him and he loved me. He kept seeing Bre and the more he saw her the more I grew hate towards her. It was easy to still play bestie since she was working more and we didn't see each other as much. When we did have our little lunch dates I would just stare at her trying to find out what it was about her that kept Drew coming back. I would beg him to leave her alone and we could be together but for some reason he couldn't. I didn't understand. But being around Bre while I was sleeping with Drew turned out to be not as hard as I thought. It was like I had an inside joke about her and I would just laugh to myself every time she brought him up. She would talk about him cheating on her and how she found messages and how he was always out in the streets. I would just think. *He doesn't even love you. He loves me. He is with ME.* After about a year I was over having to share Drew. I needed to show Drew I was loyal to him so he could see I was all he needed. I started to volunteer to help with drop offs with his drugs and money. I ended up quitting one of my jobs and helping him out in the drug game. I started stacking my money to buy my dream house for me, Anya, and Drew. I started putting pressure on Drew to leave Bre and I also pushed Bre to move on and leave Drew. I was tired of hiding and my plan was to put the pressure on them both to leave each other alone.

The day had finally come. Bre had called me and said she was finally done and left Drew. I was so relieved and happy. After we got off the phone I called Drew excited and ready to talk about where our relationship was going to go now that him and Bre were done. I was disappointed when I called him, he sounded all depressed and sad and didn't want to talk. It hurt me to know that their relationship meant that much to him. A few days had went by and he was still acting funny but I did everything I could to remind him that he had me and he didn't need Bre. I picked up extra jobs to show him I was loyal. A few days later he called me to help him with an important job. He wanted to hit up one of his enemies and rob them in the middle of them transporting their drugs. He said he was ready to move in on the competition. At first I told him I didn't want to, I had never done anything that extreme for him. All I had done was transport stuff for him. When I said no, he got upset, "How you trying to be my girl and you can't do this for me? I thought you said you loved me and was down for whatever. Ain't this what you wanted?" I wanted to prove to him I was his girl and I would do anything for him. "Ok Drew, I'll do it." So Drew, me, and a few of his crew met up to come up with a plan that same night. There was this truck driver they had been following so they could learn his routes. They learned his pick up and drop off spots so we planned on robbing him at his drop off location.

The day had come and we were following him according to plan. It was me and Drew in a black SUV and his men in another. We followed the truck driver being careful not to get noticed. The truck driver made an unscheduled stop at a truck stop that wasn't part of the route. Drew called his men that were in the other car to let them know that we were going to do it now and not at his final stop. Drew explained to me how this will be easier because the only person we would have to worry about was the truck driver and not anybody else that would have been at the drop off spot. We pulled in and parked and waited for the driver to go in the store and we pulled beside the truck. Drew had his men wait on the other side until the signal was given. When the driver came back it was on and popping. Watching Drew in action and helping load up the van and SUV was so exhilarating and such a rush. Drew was looking sexy as ever and I couldn't help but to kiss on him. He would flirt back and wink at me. He was always meant to be with me. After loading everything, we quickly got back in our cars and drove away. We were in the car hype, "See baby I told you it would be easy. We was in and out and now we got a mil in our pockets." "That was a million dollars worth of stuff!" I could finally buy my house and live the life I deserve. I screamed. My adrenaline was pumping. I put on some music to dance to.

I feel like I'm Gucci Mane in 2006
All these diamonds, dancing on my fucking neck cost like four bricks
And the way that I be totting on that strap, don't make no sense
He a million dollar n**** but be posted in the bricks. Ayy
It make no sense, yeah
It make no sense, uh
It make no sense...

(Make No Sense by NBA Young Boy)

We got home and celebrated and he gave me my cut of the money and then Drew went to Tulsa to lay low for a while. Everything was perfect. I had Drew, my soon to be house, and Bre had met someone so she was out of my hair. Life was perfect. A couple weeks had went by and there was talk on the streets about the robbery, but there wasn't any talk about who done it. I went to go visit Drew a couple times and he said he was going to stay in Tulsa for a couple more weeks. I began to get worried when Bre told me that someone had broken into her house. That part that concerned me was the fact whoever did it didn't steal anything and that it looked like they was looking for something. It was very odd that had happened in her neighborhood. I stayed with her that night to see if I could get any information from her, but she seemed completely clueless to who would have done this. I begin to get paranoid. I called Drew, "Babe something is going on. Someone broke into Bre's house, but they didn't take anything, they were just looking for something." "What?! Is Bre ok?" His comment pissed me off. He still cared about her even after everything I had done for him. I got loud, "Why do you care if she is ok? Are you still talking to her?" He sighed heavily, "No and don't start with that shit. Do she know who did it?" I let it go but I will be talking to him about it later, "No she has no idea. Did you leave anything at her house? You think whoever did it knows what we did?" "There is nothing over there and I don't know, just calm down and let me think." Drew was quiet for a second, then said, "Let me call you back but until then just chill and act normal around her." He hung up. It was Monday, the day after the break in and I was at home waiting for Drew to call me back. I started to get paranoid even more. Somebody was probably looking for Drew and if they were looking for Drew then they most likely knew I was with him that night of the robbery. What the hell am I going to do? I couldn't go to jail and if I didn't get caught by the police I would end up dead by the people we stole from. I wanted to be his ride or die but I wasn't about THAT life. While I waited for Drew to call back I decided to take Anya to her dad's house until I figured out what was going on. I was back at my place sitting on the couch stressed. I should have never gone with him that night, I should have stayed my ass at home.

Drew called me back that evening, "So word is that some guy been asking about who I am and who my girlfriend is but the people I spoke with said that they gave Bre"s name." My heart started beating fast, "So they know it was you that night? What if they find out it's not Bre and that it was me!" "Jessica, relax, I got you. They will eventually find

out it's not Bre but that doesn't mean they going to find out it is you."
I started crying and talking at the same time, "Just like they found out
it's you they will find me! I have a daughter to raise. I can't do this!"
He started yelling and getting upset, "I didn't make you do this shit,
you wanted to. I don't have time for this. You wanted to be with me so
bad, but you want to bitch and complain just like Bre would do. Now
what? You gonna abandon me like she did, like everybody else in my
life has?" I started to feel guilty and I couldn't leave him now when all
this was going on, "No, I'm not like Bre or everyone else. I'm not going
anywhere, I'm here for you." He calmed down, "All you want to do is
argue and I'm not trying to do all that, I got too much going on right
now." "You're right, I'm sorry." He asked, "Has Bre been acting
suspicious?" "No." He said, "Ok well let's just see how this plays out.
Hit me up if you hear anything." "You not coming back to the city? I
don't want to be alone, I'm scared." "Nah imma stay here but if
anything changes let me know and I'll be there." He hung up. My
emotions were everywhere, but I mostly felt hurt. For one, I can still
tell he cares about Bre and that was like a slap in the face, and two he
left me alone when he went to Tulsa. I laid down and cried myself to
sleep.

I woke up around midnight to my phone ringing. It was Bre calling
me. She sounded different. There was something wrong but she
wouldn't say. As soon as I got off the phone with her I called Drew.
"Drew wake up. Bre just called me acting weird and wants me to come
over. What the fuck am I gonna do? You need to get here now!"
"Jessica, will you please stop all that yelling, damn! I'm already
heading there I'm like an hour away." "Did something else happen?"
Something must be up since he was already heading this way. "I just
found out who the dude was that was going around town asking about
me. It's the truck driver, he goes by Blu. I lost it. "Blu?! That's the guy
Bre has been talking to! Shit! She knows!"

"What the fuck you mean? How you ain't know that shit? Ain't she your best friend?" Is he serious? "She never showed me what he looked like and I didn't know his damn name!" I continued, "She knows Drew, now that bitch is setting me up." Drew tried to calm me down, "We don't know if she knows for sure. Just call her back and tell her y'all can meet tomorrow and I will be there in a minute. For now go to a hotel and call me when you get checked in." I hung up with Drew and threw some clothes on. I texted Bre.

Jessica: Hey Bre I'm sorry I can't come tonight. I don't want to wake Anya up. We can meet tomorrow.

Bre: I really need you to come.

Jessica: I can't, sorry.

I grabbed some of the money that was left over and packed a small bag. I rushed out the door to find a hotel.

CHAPTER 17

Bre

Jessica had just text me saying that she wasn't coming. It was the first time since we were kids that she had ever not come when I needed her. We had always been there for each other no matter the time or day. This was strange because on the phone call she said she was coming and now she texted and said she wasn't, maybe her and Drew were already on the run. Maybe she knew it was a set up. I was fearing for my life right at this moment and no one could help me. My legs and hands had been untied by Blu and I was sitting in the chair with Blu, James, and his two top flight security team surrounding me. James had snatched the phone out of my hand, "You are going to take me to where your friend lives." I knew Anya was going to be there. I can't let this happen. All I said was, "Ok." I couldn't just give up and wait for them to kill me and everyone else. I added up how much time had passed since I met Blu and started seeing James as a client. It had been at least 3 weeks so the money and drugs that they were looking for were most likely gone and when he realizes that I felt for sure he would kill Jessica, Drew and me so no witnesses would be left behind. I thought about all the past conversations I had with Jessica and Blu. I remember Jessica saying how she was close to buying her house, she must had used that money she stole. I remember how Blu would ask me questions about my ex. At first I thought he was just being nosey, but now I realize he was just looking for him and trying to get information. He was so secretive about his personal life because he was married. I remember Jessica trying to turn me against Lexi when it was her being disloyal all this time. And to think all the times she encouraged me to leave Drew was only so they could be together. I was so heartbroken. I couldn't let this be the end, I didn't want to die this way. I had to think of something.

James and one of his men stepped out of the room to talk. I looked at Blu, "Look at what you've done. You thought I stole from you? And Jessica's daughter is home he is going to hurt them." Blu's eyes begin to water, "I'm sorry, I made a mistake. He is going to hurt my son if I don't get his shit back or hand Drew over to him." I wanted to say more but the other guy was standing there watching us. Blu looked like he was thinking about something. I started to try to think of a plan but all I could think was if I don't take them to Jessica's house they will kill me and if I did take them there they will kill me, her and Anya. All the men in the world and she had to pick him. I just shook my head. The thought of it made me sick to my stomach. I at least hope she sensed something was wrong and took Anya and herself somewhere else. James walked back into the room, "All of you, come with me now." James turned around and walked out the room and the guy that was in the room with us motioned for me and Blu to follow behind. I stood up and Blu walked out the room first with me behind him and the other guy behind me. James and his security had their backs to us walking towards the door. I wondered how far I would make it if I was to run. Blu had stopped walking which made me stop. I watched Blu reach under his shirt and into his pants and pull out a gun and put it to James' head. The other two guys pulled out their guns. The one behind me had his gun on me and the other guy had his gun on Blu. Blu grabbed James and spun him around so that they were facing all of us. I was so still I was holding my breath. Blu had a hold of James by the neck with his gun to his head. James spoke first, "I see you didn't forget your gun this time." Blu ignored him, "You two put your guns on the table now," Blu ordered. They didn't move. Blu yelled, "Put the guns on the table now!" James nodded his head at his crew and they did as they were told. I was terrified. I looked around taking in what was happening and I saw my keys on the kitchen counter. Blu reached into James pants and pulled out his gun and put it in his pocket. Blu then ordered them to put their cell phones on the table also and then told them to stand back in the corner away from us and the guns. "Bre get a trash bag and put the guns and the other phones in them. I glanced at the keys again. *Just grab them and go. Go. Leave him.* Blu saw me hesitate, "Bre I know you don't trust me, but let me make this right. Please." This time he was pleading with me like I was when I was tied up. I couldn't trust him. Fuck him. I grabbed my keys and phone and ran like a bat out of a cave out the door to the garage. I hit the button to open the garage door and got in my car and left.

I had no clue to where I was going or what I was going to do. I found myself heading to Jessica's place. I needed to confront her. I needed her to see the mess she has caused. And I was going to make her tell me where Drew was. I prayed she hadn't had spent all of that crazy man's money. I pulled to her place and no one was there. I knew that meant she knew. And like a coward she was running. I could have easily gave them her address, but I didn't, and to see she had left me knowing they could possibly kill me was painful. I was at least happy to know Anya was safe. I pulled off and continued driving until I stopped at an empty parking lot. I parked and turned off my engine and I cried for a few minutes not knowing what to do. There was a small part of me concerned for Blu and his son. He set me up in hopes to save his son. It didn't make the situation right, but I could understand doing what you have to do for your child. Anya wasn't my child but I was there the moment she was born until now and I loved her and would die if something happened to her. I took a deep breath and called Lexi. Maybe she could help me. Lexi answered on the first ring, "Bre I'm glad you called, we need to talk, I miss you, I miss us....wait what you doing up this late?" I started crying, "I miss you too." "Bre, what's wrong?" I just cried and cried. These last two days had been the worst days of my life. My house had been broken into, I had been tied up and beaten, and all behind the hands of an ex and a guy I cared about. Lexi interrupted my crying, "I'm on my way over." "No, I'm not at home." "Where the hell are you?" I told Lexi the short version of what all has happened. "Ooooh hell no! We about to beat her ass right neowwww." "I just left her place and she not there. I don't know where she is." "Ok just come to my place and we will figure this out." "Ok." I hung up and started my car back up. Just to think a couple days ago Jessica had me feeling like I needed to stop being her friend. I don't think I would be able to trust again. I heard some tires screeching in the background. I looked in my rearview mirror and it was Blu. *How the hell did he find me?* He parked blocking me in and hopped out the car. He ran to my door. "Bre please listen to me, they could be close. They are tracking you." He kneeled down and reached under my car. "Blu what the hell are you doing?" He stood back up with a device in his hand. My mouth was wide open, it was starting to come together. The day I met him in the parking lot he said he was looking for his mask. He lied and put some type of location tracker on my car and that's how he knew where I was downtown Saturday night. I opened the door and got out of the car. "You put a tracker on my car?" I swung at him and he grabbed and restrained me. He held me up against the car. "I thought you were Drew's girlfriend, I thought it was you that night at the truck stop with him. I didn't see the video until after they tied you up and I realized I had made a mistake. They can track you too. They could be on their way here now. We don't have time. We gotta go!" I was now panicking, "Just leave my car?" "Yes, we gotta go!" I grabbed my keys and phone and we left my car with the tracker there. I got in the car with Blu and we sped off.

In the back seat of Blu's car was his mom and son. "Bre this is my mom, Johnnie and my son Jaxon. Jaxon was laid out on the seat half asleep and Blu's mom was going off. "Kenneth, I can't believe you got yourself in this mess. Bre I am so sorry he got you into this mess, I raised him better than this and I am so disappointed." I looked at Blu, "Kenneth?" He answered, "Kenneth is my first name, I go by Blu." "Is there anything else you have lied about? Now is the time to get everything out." He thought for a second, "Me and my wife are separated and going through a divorce. She is an unfit mother and I couldn't leave this earth without fighting for my son. I can't leave him with her." Johnnie threw in her two cents, "And I wasn't going to let that hoe raise MY grandson anyway. I won't allow it." As much as I didn't want to believe him, I did. Blu drove until he got to a hotel. He set up a room for his mom and son. We got them settled into their room. "Kenneth, you get this shit taken care of. You got me and Jaxon out late up in this damn hotel like the police is looking for us or somethin'. Then you lying to this young lady. You just like yo crazy ass daddy and you over here with that same stupid face he would have when he knew he had fucked up. I should slap yo ass right back to the moment you had me fucked up for waking me up and having us in this damn hotel." His mom was letting him have it and I was here for it. "Mom, relax, I will take care of everything like I always do. I'm sorry I have you out late, I'm sorry for everything, I just wanted to make sure you and Jaxon were going to be safe." She sighed and threw her hands up and put Jaxon to bed. Blu hugged and kissed his mom and son and told them he loved them and we left. Walking through the lobby Lexi called, I answered, "My bad some shit just went down but I'm on my way to your place now." I could hear music in the background and it sounded like she was in her car driving. She responded, "I know where Jessica is."

CHAPTER 18

Bre

He hit his arm just before he pulled the trigger. If it had been one second earlier, he would have been gone. They started wrestling on the ground, fighting for the gun. He had him pinned down, his forearm was on his throat. He tried reaching for the gun. I was screaming, "Please stop." I didn't know what to do. They both lunged for the gun. She yelled for me to get on the ground. We kneeled beside the car. I closed my eyes tight and said a prayer. Two shots went off....

Me and Blu had just left the hotel. Lexi told us that her cousin who works at a Holiday Inn Express said she saw Jessica check-in there. So that's where we were headed and Lexi was meeting us there. I was staring out the window wondering what I would do if I saw Jessica. I was feeling vengeful. I was angry and hurt. I saw my best friend kiss my ex and the way she did it you could tell there was love and passion behind it. They had to have been together while we were together. I got sick to my stomach again thinking about it. Blu interrupted my thoughts, "I know an apology won't make this better and I know you think everything was fake but it wasn't. I do care about you." Blu was trying his best to make amends. I was still upset. "You lied about so much. Was not telling me about you being married part of the plan to set me up?" He shook his head, "I wanted to be honest but at the time I didn't know how you would react. I really thought it was you that had robbed me the whole time." "Really? Even after you got to know me a little more? I fit the profile of someone who robs people for drugs and money?" He looked at me, "People lie. Just like Jessica did. I'm sure she didn't fit the profile either." That comment pissed me off, "Fuck you. If we survive this shit you got us into, Imma need you to act like we never met." He sighed, "Don't be that way. There was something that told me it wasn't you but I wasn't sure. James had someone watching my son. All he had to do was make a phone call and my son would have been killed. I had to follow through with it and I didn't see the video until after you were tied up. I'm telling you the truth. You left me at your house with James and his men. I was able to get away and I could have left town with my son and mom and not look back but I didn't. I went looking for you, I knew James would come for you." I didn't say anything. I didn't know what to say. We both was quiet the rest of the way.

We pulled into the Holiday Inn Express. I texted Lexi and told her what car we were in. A minute went by and she text back and said she was walking up. Lexi hopped in the back seat and we hugged, "Are you ok?" She asked, concerned. "No," I said honestly. "I'm sorry I haven't been a good friend lately but I'm here now and we about to drag this bitch." I smiled. I introduced Blu to Lexi. "Mmm so you're Blu. You know after we drag Jessica we gonna drag you right?" "I deserve it, but that's not going to happen." Lexi looked at me, "Oh I like him. You hit that?" Lexi kept talking. She didn't realize something else had caught my attention. Right in front of me about two rows away I saw Jessica and Drew getting bags out the car. I felt so many emotions, but mostly rage. I saw red. It was like a wall of fire before my eyes and I felt a fire burning inside. I couldn't hear Lexi and Blu talking anymore. I couldn't hear anything but my heart beating and my slowed breaths. I didn't realize I had gotten out of the car and was walking towards them. Then I started running. I was running but everything felt like slow motion. Drew and Jessica was so into each other's presence that when they noticed me it was too late. I kicked Drew in the nuts and he fell into the fetal position. Then I went for Jessica. Pop. Right punch to the nose. Pop. Left punch to the cheek. She fought back but was too slow and dazed from the two blows that caught her off guard. She lost her balance and fell and pulled me with her. I saw other punches flying. Lexi had joined in on the ass whooping. Jessica managed to kick me off of her. I fell back and got back up. A quick glance and I could see Blu was giving it to Drew. He was tearing his ass up and talking to him, "Where your gun at now?" Jessica managed to get up but Lexi had her by the hair and Jessica was throwing punches at her. I still saw fire. I got back at it. Lexi let go of her hair and me and Jessica squared up. "I been waiting for this," Jessica said. That threw me off. Somewhere over the years my best friend stopped being my best friend. She had been waiting to fight me. She had been waiting for this moment which confirms she and Drew been together for a while. We charged each other like bulls. Lexi was in the background, "That's right, beat that ass up good." I heard police sirens in the background. Blu grabbed me off of Jessica, "We gotta go." I looked at Drew. He was laying on the ground. His nose was bloody and he had a knot on his head. He slowly got off the ground and went to his car. I knew what that meant. It meant it was time to go. We ran back to the car that was still running and sped off. I looked through the back window and Drew had his gun pointed at us but we were already turning out the parking lot. Lexi was amped up, "Biiiiittchhh I didn't know you and Mike Tyson was 1st cousins. You was giving her all business and that's on PERIODDTTT. It be the quiet ones that be knowing how to fight." I asked out of breath, "Lexi, you cool if we go to your place?" "Nah not at all." Lexi gave Blu her address. Blu was pretty quiet. "Blu you ok?" "Yeah I'm just mad it escalated so fast. We didn't get to ask about the money or I at least wanted to bring him to James." Blu was stressed, hell I was too. We still had to figure out what we were going to do about this James situation. He for damn sure wasn't going to just let it go. I felt my phone vibrating, I checked it. It was Jessica. I hit the talk button and didn't even have to say hello Jessica was already yelling, "Bitch best believe if I wouldn't had got jumped I would have whooped yo ass but how does it feel to see your man with me. He loves me. We been together for almost two years and your dumbass was clueless the whole time." She laughed and continued, "It's your fault though you ran him off to someone better. Me." Jessica sounded like a lunatic, "Jessica, what did I do to deserve this? You were my best friend." "Save that shit. It was all about your career and Lexi. I deserved Drew. You didn't and that's why." "Jessica there are people that are going to kill us, all of us, if you don't give them their shit back." "We good over here so not my problem. My man will protect us." "James knew it was you and Drew. So it is your problem and what about Anya?" She hung up. I wanted to cry, but I had no tears left. I wanted to scream, but I had no energy left. "Don't worry about her she will get her karma," Lexi said as she rubbed my shoulder." Blu spoke, "We're being followed."

CHAPTER 19

Blu

We were headed to Lexi's house and after a couple turns I noticed a black SUV following us. I knew exactly who it was. When we were at Bre's house, after she left, I took their guns and phones. Before I took them I made James call his crew and call off the watch of my son. I then made them get undressed and I threw their clothes in my trunk with the guns and phones. James was furious. What I did was the ultimate disrespect and I knew he wanted me dead. I knew he was hunting for me and he had found me. He probably didn't even care about his money and drugs anymore. He could make that back in a couple days. I had to think of something. Bre and Lexi started panicking and I had exited off the highway. I increased my speed and so did they. I weaved in and out between cars and so did they. They got beside us and tried to force me off the side of the road. I swerved over to the other lane almost hitting another car but I was able to get back in control. I pushed on the gas a little more and tried to lose them. Lexi was yelling out orders, "Turn here. Hurry!" Bre was trying to brace herself for every turn. They were right behind us. They rear ended us. Lexi yelled, "Go faster!" "I can't, you don't see these cars around us!" This was not like in the movies or video games. This was real life and I had to try to get away without hitting other people and wrecking. They got beside us again and this time with a little more force they ran us off the road. We went up a curve and onto some grass and hit a pole. I hit my head on the window and was a little dazed. I looked at Bre and Lexi, "Y'all ok?" "Yeah" they said together. They were a little bit in shock. Crash! Kash and Ben had broken my driver side window. They reached in and opened the door and pulled me out. I fell on the ground and the two started throwing punches and kicks. I felt shooting pain everywhere. Bre had got out of the car and came to where we were and jumped on Kash, he slung her off him like she was a rag doll. James appeared and they stopped beating me. I laid there eyes swollen and lip busted. And I'm sure I had a broken rib. James walked up to me, pulled out his gun, and pointed it at me. He looked me in my eyes, smiled and said, "Your son and mom will be next." POW. Tears ran down my face. I closed my eyes and accepted death. I didn't feel any pain. I was still breathing. I opened my eyes. James had a bullet hole in his head. He fell to the floor. Pow. Pow. Two more shots. One for Kash and one for Ben. I was confused. I looked at Bre on the ground and she was staring at Lexi, mouth opened completely shocked. I got up off the ground and turned to see Lexi in the back seat with a 9mm in her hand. "Y'all get the fuck up and let's go!" Like a robot on auto pilot I got back in the driver's side and Bre got back in the car also. I was still trying to put two and two together. I checked to see if my gun was still in the middle console and it was and I knew the other guns were in the trunk. I knew Bre didn't have a gun. So that meant that was Lexi's gun. Who the hell is this chic? Thankfully, the car was still drivable and we drove away. We left their bodies there. Was this really happening in my life? Just a month ago me and my son was eating cereal with our underwear on watching cartoons and now here I am with three dead bodies around me. Bre was going off on Lexi, "Lexi where you get that gun and how you know how to shoot like that? You killed them so easily. I can't believe you did that! Have you done this before?" Bre was turned around in her seat looking at Lexi. We both waited on her to answer because I wanted to know too. "I was raised in the streets and my daddy made sure I knew how to shoot and made sure I always kept a gun." Me and Bre were quiet and she added, "I wasn't going to let them kill him." The look on Bre's face showed that she didn't know her friends like she thought. "Lexi you just killed 3 men and you seem so calm about it. You're scaring me right now." "Bre, it was either them or us. You think they was going to let us just walk away after we watched them kill Blu?" She was right, she saved all our lives. Damn. I looked at her through the rearview mirror, "Thank you." "You're welcome and we need to pull up at a car wash real quick and wash the car." Me and Bre both looked at each other surprised. She definitely seen or done some shit. We drove to a car wash and washed my car. I couldn't believe that James was dead. I had worked these last couple years with him making money. His whole operation saved me and my family from poverty and in a blink of an eye, he was dead. The relationship me and James had built with each other didn't mean anything though, he was ready to kill me and my family. I had understood the law of the streets but could I had really prevented Drew from robbing me? And if I did who is to say Drew wouldn't have found another way. Either way this life wasn't for me. I had never seen anyone get shot before and I had never seen anybody die right in front of my eyes before. As I washed the car I kept having flashes of their bodies falling to the ground and I can't believe I was that close to death. When he pulled the gun on me, I knew for sure I was about to take my last breath. Lexi had saved my life and I would forever be in debt to her. Lexi and Bre were standing by the car watching me wash it. Lexi was holding Bre telling her that it was ok and it was all over. Even though our big problem had been taken care of, I knew after the way I beat Drew up he would be coming for me because he wouldn't be able to accept an ass whooping like a man. And even though I didn't kill anybody, I was still an accessory to murder. Now I have to watch my back from Drew and pray the police don't find us. When we had been run off the road only one car had passed by and with it being late at night on a weekday nobody was out and about. Lexi said, "We were all three at my place the whole night tonight and I'll have my neighbor vouch for that." "You think I should get rid of my car?" "Yeah that would be safe." Lexi got in the car. I walked over to Bre. You could tell her mind was going a million miles per minute. I hugged her and she held me back. She said, "What are we going to do?" "Everything will be ok." I was telling myself that too. Lexi yelled out the window, "We need to go before we be seen." We hopped in the car and headed to my place first to switch out my car. I pulled it in the garage and we headed to Lexi's. As we drove, Lexi assured us that she would take care of everything. Me and Bre sat quietly while Lexi made some phone calls. She mostly talked in code so it was hard to understand but I'm sure she had gave the location of the bodies. We all sat quietly the rest of the way. "Turn right here." Lexi pointed at the upcoming street. We pulled into her apartments and she guided me to her building and we parked.

Chapter 20

Bre

Lexi was a motha fuckin gangsta. As we drove to the car wash I thought about how I didn't really know my friends like I thought. I looked at Jessica as someone who was strong minded and independent, but turns out she was the complete opposite. She needed to steal to make a way and she was weak enough to allow Drew to manipulate her into doing whatever he wanted. I was guilty of being manipulated by him also but there was no way I was getting involved with any illegal activity. I used to think Lexi couldn't take care of herself and was irresponsible, but I looked at her all wrong. She obviously could handle herself. I judged her for using men and taking the easy way out but she was actually independent and strong. She was who she was, a girl from the streets, that didn't take no shit and was always hustling.

We pulled into the car wash and we all got out. Blu started washing the car. Even with everything going on I couldn't help but still feel that same attraction for him. Watching him wash the car, I thought about our night together. I'm happy he came to find me after I left him at my house. James would have tracked me down and killed me for sure. Lexi walked up to me, "Are you ok? I'm sorry you had to see that." "Lexi I am grateful you saved us but sis, where did this come from?" "My family was part of a big drug cartel in Texas and Oklahoma. I was raised in it. He taught me how to shoot, hustle, and how to be smart about my decisions. I know you think I'm some immature female chasing men and money but the truth is I have $20 million sitting in four different banks, two that's overseas. I don't have a job because I don't want one and I don't need one and don't worry about your house, I'll get you a new one." *Did this bitch say $20 million?* "But why didn't you ever mention this to me?" "So you would have wanted me to say hi I'm Lexi and I am the daughter of an infamous drug lord and I'm sitting on $20 million?" "Uh, yeah, that actually would have been nice." She laughed, "Yeah right, you probably wouldn't had been my friend, and if you did stick around I wouldn't trust you was my actual friend or if you were using me for my money. I keep that information about me quiet for protection." I understood, but was still sad she didn't feel comfortable telling me after all this time. "Everyone has been lying to me, Jessica, Blu, and now you." She hugged me, "I know and I'm sorry, but know that I would never do no shady shit like Jessica did." She hugged me and told Blu what our alibi would be and got in the car. My mind was blown. She had fooled me and Jessica. She had even asked us for money a few times just to cover up the fact she had millions. Blu had walked up to me and hugged me and told me that everything was going to be ok. His hug was so comforting and I had missed it.

We got back in the car and went to Blu's house to switch cars. "Hold up so you don't live in that apartment? You live in this big ass house?" "I completely forgot about that. That apartment was one of James' properties that he let me use." I just shook my head, "Wow you had me in that small ass apartment and I could have been over here." Blu gave me a look as if to say give me a break. I just rolled my eyes. I was so done with the lies, as soon as I thought I knew everything there was another surprise. We drove to Lexi's place. It was a quiet ride for the most part other than the phone calls she made. Lexi was a *motha fuckin gangsta*. We got to her building and parked. Before we got out of the car Lexi said, "We are going to chill here for a while until I make a few phone calls and then I'm going to see what the streets are saying." At this point whatever she says goes, neither me nor Blu questioned her. Lexi lived in some decent apartments. They wasn't

102

old or run down in a bad neighborhood, but they wasn't the nicest. It was almost four in the morning and the sun would be coming up soon. I couldn't wait to sit down and take a deep breath. We had been going nonstop all night. Me and Blu followed behind Lexi as we walked to her apartment. As we was walking he grabbed my hand and held it. He looked at me and smiled. I saw his dimple and couldn't help but smile back. He kissed my hand. We had been through a lot and seen a lot, probably him more so than me. Situations like that could bring people closer. We both was as close to death as it could get tonight and I felt closer to him. *Maybe I could forgive him.* We walked and stared at each other as we were approaching her building. He looked away. Something had caught his attention. Behind the bushes next to her building Drew jumped out and was right in front of us. Drew had a gun and was aiming at Blu and in a blink of an eye Blu slapped his arm and knocked the gun out his hand. They started fighting and wrestling on the ground. Lexi pulled out her gun but a crowd was starting to form outside. People heard the scuffling and were either looking out their windows or coming outside. Drew shook Blu loose and he tried to crawl towards the gun. Blu grabbed him by his foot and pulled him towards him and got on top of him. Blu pinned him down with his forearm on his throat. He tried reaching for the gun but couldn't quite get it. "Please stop!" I was going to go for the gun but Lexi grabbed me. Blu used his strength and pushed off of Drew. Drew was able to turn over on all fours and crawl. They both went for the gun. Lexi pulled me down, "Get on the ground!" We fell to the ground by a car. I closed my eyes and said a prayer. Two shots went off. Pow. Pow. I looked up. Drew and Blu were laying on the floor. "Blu?" Neither one of them were moving. "Blu!" I got up and ran towards them. I yelled again, "Blu!" Please God. Please. Please. Let him be ok. I could hear Lexi in the background talking to 911. This can't be real.

CHAPTER 21

Bre

December 2020

If you got it, it aint no question
No it aint no room for guessing
No more than emotionally invested
Showing you all my imperfections
                    (Damage by H.E.R.)

I was driving, listening to music. I just left from seeing Jaxon and Johnnie. None of us had been doing well since Blu died that night in front of Lexi's apartment. Drew had got up, grabbed his gun, and ran. There was blood everywhere coming from Blu's chest. I performed CPR the best I could until the ambulance arrived, but he had died instantly from two bullets to the heart. I was devastated. I had to drive back to the hotel and tell his mom and son that he was gone. I will never forget the look in his mom's eyes and the scream she let out. When she opened the door to her room and saw me standing there with blood all over my clothes, she knew immediately. I was happy when Lexi paid for the funeral because I was feeling survivors guilt. The ceremony was beautiful. After the funeral Jaxon's mother got all his money and it didn't take long for her to run through it all. Word was she was now prostituting herself and strung out on drugs. I had stepped in to help Johnnie whenever I could. I helped her with Jaxon and watched him sometimes so she could get a break. Jaxon was such a cute kid and well behaved. I made sure to set him up with therapy to deal with the loss of his dad and also to deal with not having a good mother around.

Holding me tight, Loving me right, Giving me life
All night you could be
Telling me lies, Making me cry, Wasting my time the whole time
So Just be careful what you take for granted, yeah
Cause with me you know you could do damage
                                        (Damage by H.E.R.)

After that night at Lexi's, word had got out that Drew was responsible for James, Kash, and Ben's death. A week after Blu died, Drew was found sitting in his car parked at Lake Hefner with a bullet to his head. It was said to be a gang retaliation by police. Drew killed James and James' men put a hit out on Drew. I asked Lexi did she have anything to do with putting the word out about Drew killing James. She rolled her eyes and said, "You in my business? Don't do that." I knew she did. I was happy she did. It would have been a believable story. The news story read, 'Two big time drug dealers fighting over territory and killed each other." I don't know how Lexi did it but I was relieved to know I wouldn't have to look over my shoulder wondering if the police would be knocking at my door. I was also hurt that four black men had died due to a country and system that had failed us. Although a great deal of responsibility lies within ourselves there are other factors that come into play. Drew died from a vicious cycle of broken families that lead to the streets raising him and the search of love and acceptance from gangs. Blu died from a system that was determined to keep minorities poor and from gaining any wealth. Being born black means you are already a few steps behind in gaining financial security, so that means you have to work harder than the majority while facing unfair obstacles. Although I don't know James' story, I know he has one. We all do.

Jessica was six months pregnant with Drew's baby. She was going around town blaming me for Drew's death and bragging how she took my man and was having his baby. I was still hurt, but I was mostly sad for her because you had to be a miserable person to think that way and do what she did. She would harass me by calling and texting me after Drew died, but I put a stop to that quick. I changed my number and blocked her on all social media. We had nothing to talk about. Our friendship was over and I didn't care what she said about me or what other people thought about me. I just prayed for her. I missed Anya, but I decided to make the hard decision and not have her in my life. I prayed for her the most and hoped she wouldn't grow up to be like her mama. Lexi said she had ran into her a month ago at Penn Square Mall and she looked smoked out and depressed. Lexi said as soon as she saw her she ran the other way. Lexi kept her word and helped me get a house. I went back that next day and my car was in perfect condition, but I felt uneasy driving it, so I sold it and got a cherry Range Rover. Me and Lexi had gotten close and she had opened up more to me. It turns out she had a sad story as well. She opened up about her childhood and her traumas and all the things that made her who she was today. I now understood why she kept things so secretive. I was dealing with the trauma from the events from that night. I was depressed and I was suffering from anxiety. I also had nightmares every night. I was deeply sad about losing Blu. I would never know what we could have had. Deep down I knew he was the one and I feared that I would never find that chemistry with someone else again. I parked and walked to my building, but this time I went to a different room instead of my own suite. I sat on a couch and in front of me was my new therapist. "So Bre, what are some things you would like to accomplish through therapy." I took a deep breath and let it all out...

Hebrews 13:5-6

Your trauma may look different compared to others, but it is real.
Acknowledge it, seek help, and let it end with you.

—Chastae'

Made in the USA
Coppell, TX
23 March 2021

52219991R00069